MURDER,
LONDON – SOUTH AFRICA

By the same author in PAN Books

JOHN CREASEY

MURDER,
LONDON – SOUTH AFRICA

UNABRIDGED

PAN BOOKS LTD : LONDON

First published 1966 by Hodder and Stoughton Ltd.

This edition published 1968 by Pan Books Ltd.,
33 Tothill Street, London, S.W.1

330 02198 2

Printed and bound in England by
Hazell Watson & Viney Ltd.
Aylesbury, Bucks

CONTENTS

I

MISSING MAN

'Handsome in?'

'No.'

'Anyone seen Handsome?'

'Not since lunch.'

'Handsome. Handsome! Anyone seen Handsome?'

'If I had a nickname like Handsome I'd want to hang myself,' said a middle-aged detective-sergeant at New Scotland Yard. 'It's bad enough looking like a film-star, let alone being called like one. Handsome, Handsome, anyone seen Handsome?' he mimicked.

'Is someone asking for me?' inquired Chief Superintendent Roger 'Handsome' West of the Criminal Investigation Department. He was irritated, but he knew the sergeant for a somewhat disappointed and consequently jaundiced man, and bore him no ill-will, so he did not reveal the fact that he had heard everything the other had said as he approached a corner of a passage in the offices on the Embankment. He looked inquiringly into Sergeant Gorlay's startled grey eyes.

Gorlay was quick of thought as well as movement, a lean ferret of a man. He drew himself up to an attitude almost of attention, so as to emphasize respect.

'Good afternoon, sir. Yes. There has been a call for you. I believe that you're wanted in the Assistant Commissioner's office.'

'Mustn't keep him waiting, must we,' said Roger, and he lengthened his stride towards his own office. As the door opened, the sound of his telephone bell came clearly along the passage, and the door closed on his 'hallo'. The man with Gorlay, another detective-sergeant, grinned and said:

'Handsome is as Handsome does. He couldn't have failed to hear you.'

'Could have,' Gorlay conceded.

In his office, Roger sat on the corner of his desk, glancing at four reports which had been put there since he had left only half an hour ago. A shaft of October sunlight, reflected from the River Thames, shimmered on a section of the dark, shiny desk. The office was at its brightest, for there had been hardly a cloud over London's sky all day.

'You're through,' the operator said.

'West here,' said Roger. 'Is that right you've been after me?'

'If you'd been away much longer I would have wanted to know where you'd been,' retorted the Assistant Commissioner gruffly. 'Come along right away, will you?'

He rang off before Roger could say another word. Roger stood up from the desk, but did not go immediately to the door. He moved to the window and looked past the bright green of the leaves of the plane trees on the Embankment, and the traffic, towards the broad river beyond, and the mass of London County Hall on the farther side. He was not thinking about the river scene, nor even of the sun. He was telling himself that first Gorlay and now Hardy had made him feel angry, and that was a bad sign. He had covered his irritation with the sergeant just as he must with the Assistant Commissioner, but he needed a minute or two's respite and he would need more than minutes to analyse his feelings.

Was there any justification for feeling mad? Wouldn't he have laughed off both things only a few weeks ago?

He turned away from the day's brightness and went out. He moved as he always did, with a kind of restrained briskness, as if he knew exactly where he wanted to go but something prevented him going too fast. The Assistant Commissioner's office was upstairs; it wasn't worth taking the lift. By the time he had climbed the stairs he was actually hurrying. Doubtless Hardy had been annoyed by something, too. Probably, he would be back to normal when Roger arrived. On the other hand, for a senior officer at the Yard to be told that he might have to explain where he had been for half an hour—

Roger began to smile. He had been out to lunch. With his wife. On a working weekday. That was little more than an annual event. He reached Hardy's office, and was about to tap when caution made him go on to the secretary's room, next door. Hardy was a man of moods and there was no point in exacerbating the situation. He went inside, and a middle-aged woman, who was bending over a typewriter, glanced up. It was obvious at once that she was out of temper, too; she usually had a smile which brightened her homely but pleasant face. Now she said:

'The Assistant Commissioner would like you to go straight in.'

'Thanks.' Often Roger would have asked her what was up, but today he decided that it would not be wise. So he tapped at the communicating door, and as he did so the keys of the typewriter began to clatter, as if snapping out a coded message of defiance.

Hardy was at his big, dark, shiny pedestal-type desk, with its In, Out, Pending, and other trays. The office was not large, but there was room for more chairs, more furniture, more filing-cabinets. The bareness gave it a look of austerity, and in a way there was a look of austerity about Hardy, too. He was an aloof man, one who had come up from the ranks and had been given this eminence because no one better was available at the time. Sometimes he gave the impression that he was as soured as Gorlay, but Roger was never sure this was so. Hardy was probably a lonely man, not quite big enough for his job. He was not heavily-built, as old-time Yard men went, but rather spare-boned, dressed in neutral grey, giving the impression that he was a little too well-brushed. He had a rather broad face and deep-set eyes. All his features were good in themselves, but the assemblage wasn't particularly striking, rather as though everything had been done by an indifferent artist.

'So you made it.' Hardy was frowning.

'Sorry I'm late,' Roger said. 'I'd no idea you wanted to see me this afternoon.'

'Couldn't very well. I didn't know myself.'

Suddenly the frown disappeared, Hardy squared his

shoulders and drew in a deep breath, as if mentally he was pushing something aside. Bad humour?

'I've had urgent instructions from the Commissioner. There's some kind of trouble over at South Africa House, and he wants you to go and find out what it's all about.' It would have been easy for Hardy to say that this was because he, Roger, had been assigned to a number of cases with overseas angles, and had proved to have a flair for getting on with people and policemen whose outlook was very different from most in Great Britain. Hardy did not take the opportunity, implying rather that he was sending Roger to South Africa House because he had been told to, not because he thought he was the right man for the job. He added: 'Go over there at once, will you? The man you want to see is a Mr du Toit, the Consul-General if I understood him properly.'

'Do you know what it's all about?' asked Roger.

'Someone left South Africa for London and didn't get here. There's a pall of secrecy for some reason – and I don't know whether the Commissioner knows more than I do and didn't choose to tell me, or whether he's as much in the dark as I am. You're to go because of your well-known discretion,' Hardy added, and there was no doubt at all of the sarcasm in his voice.

Roger contemplated him, biting back a comment, and then turned towards the door, saying:

'Sometimes that gets stretched a bit too far.'

Hardy asked sharply:

'What does?'

'My discretion. Incidentally—' Roger reached the door leading to the secretary's office, half opened it, and said clearly: 'I took my wife out to lunch today.' He paused long enough to give Hardy a chance to disapprove, but the senior man didn't take it. Roger went out, and the door closed. At least Hardy's secretary had thawed a little, and she stopped typing.

'You wouldn't know what I've done wrong, would you?' Roger asked.

'I don't even know what *I've* done wrong!'

Roger smiled ... and was chuckling by the time he reached his own office. He had counted four fresh files on his desk twenty minutes ago; now there were eight. He picked up his briefcase, pushed all the files in, and went out immediately. He wouldn't need his murder-bag – at least, he hardly expected to. He walked along the corridor to the sergeants' office, and saw Gorlay and two others, each busy at high desks; form-filling was a kind of plague at the Yard.

Gorlay looked up, and started.

'Tell the operator that I'll be out for an hour or more, will you? And I may have to telephone for my bag – if I do, bring it by car to South Africa House. If you're not around make sure someone is.'

'Right, sir!'

Roger went along the corridors and out the back way, across the Yard, into Parliament Street, and then along Whitehall. It was a wonderful Indian summer, and he was wearing a light-weight suit which he had bought in Australia only the previous year; it wasn't often he had a chance to use it here at home.

Whitehall, the colour of its older buildings neutralized by the bright sun, had a kind of splendour which it was hard to forget and yet easy not to notice. He wondered why he was acutely aware of it now – its breadth, the distant view, the sight of Nelson atop his column, the newer buildings which in themselves seemed so stark and bare, yet which somehow merged with the old ministry buildings. He went past the Horse Guards where a hundred or so late-season tourists stood staring at two guardsmen sitting still as statues on their black horses, red cloaks and burnished helmets a reminder of dead glories. Dead? Roger saw the sweep of Trafalgar Square, glanced across at the Admiralty Arch and down the Mall, which looked cool and beautifully green. Dead glories? Were they so dead?

He now knew why he was thinking so much about them and not noticing so much today. It had nothing to do with the tourists or the clicking cameras; it was because of the way his thoughts had quickened when he had been told there was a problem in South Africa House. If one looked up

South Africa in a gazetteer, one found it listed under 'Foreign Countries', but somehow that seemed wrong, whatever one might think politically. In fact, of course, it was very difficult to think of South Africa without being influenced by the background of the politics which had brought about the change from 'Commonwealth' to 'Foreign'.

He crossed Trafalgar Square at the end of the Strand, and turned towards the massive building on the right. He went in. The hall was cool and spacious, and the commissionaire as Cockney as any London policeman; in fact, he *was* the next best thing to a member of the Force, and when he recognized Roger he drew himself up much as Gorlay had done.

'Afternoon, Mr West!'

'Hallo, Baker – couldn't get into another uniform quick enough, I see.' Roger saw the half-proffered hand, and shook it, callouses and all. 'You can't have been away more than a year.'

'Two and a half years, sir. Amazing how time flies, isn't it? It wasn't so much the money,' he confided. 'It was doing nothing that got me down. Live in a flat, you see. My wife can look after the window-box, and she soon got tired of having me about the house. Who do you want to see, sir?'

Roger almost told him, but the inborn caution, which made the difference between a born policeman and merely a good one, stepped in, and he grinned.

'Public Relations – I forget the chap's name.'

'Mr Morgan that would be, sir. Second floor. Take the lift, and . . .'

It seemed to Roger that Baker's voice was still echoing in his ears when he reached the Public Relations office. He was welcomed into a magnificently-walled room, with panelling rather like an ocean liner's, by a pleasant-looking, well-groomed young woman.

'Oh, Mr du Toit's on the next floor, sir. You've been misdirected. If you'll come this way . . .'

She had a slight accent, a pleasant perfume, a friendly and natural manner. By the time he reached an office marked *Consul-General – Inquiries*, Roger's mood was very much better than it had been since he had first heard Gorlay.

When a middle-aged man asked if he had an appointment he realized that, whatever the reason for his visit, it wasn't widely known; it was a good thing he had been careful. He was led by one secretary to a second, and finally into another richly-panelled room, with high windows and a high ceiling; one wall carved with wild animals, the opposite wall with covered wagons and men and women in olden-day dress. From a desk larger than Hardy's and set in front of the main window, a very tall man stood up. Roger had a curious impression that the man was watching him almost with suspicion, certainly with wariness. Yet his manner could not have been more pleasant; his voice was also very slightly accented. He was probably older than he looked, which was about thirty-five.

He shook hands, and motioned to a leather-seated arm-chair.

'Please sit down, Mr West ... A cigarette? ... So you are cutting down on smoking; nearly everyone seems to be.' Du Toit waited for Roger to sit, went back to his own chair, and placed his hands on the desk in front of him, the fingers linked. 'Mr West, I am indeed glad to meet you, and to know that you have been selected for this very delicate task. A man of very great prominence in South Africa left Johannesburg by air four days ago. It is believed that he reached London Airport on Monday, but since then no one has any idea where he may have gone. I think I should say at once that we do not believe he would have disappeared of his own accord. I am sure you see our problem.'

2

MYSTERY

ROGER DID not answer immediately, partly because he did not quite know what to say, partly because he wanted time to try to sum up the man as well as the situation. As he sat appraising du Toit, he realized there was a third factor: simply that he was not considering this in the way he would in Australia House, or even the United States Embassy. He did not believe that du Toit's counterpart in either place would watch him so intently; almost warily.

Du Toit waited until it almost became a test of who could stay silent the longer. Slowly, Roger found himself relaxing, and he smiled faintly as he said:

'I see a little of the problem.'

'I will give you all the details which we have so far, including' – du Toit placed his right hand on a pale-pink folder – 'the report from our Pretoria and Johannesburg police headquarters.'

'One basic thing first,' Roger said.

'Yes?'

'Is this a political matter?'

Du Toit did not stir in his chair, but it seemed to Roger that the pressure of his hand on the reports suddenly became much firmer.

'Would it make any difference to you, as an official of the Metropolitan Police, if it were political?'

'As a policeman, of course not. As a person it might, and the trouble is that the two sometimes overlap.'

'At least you admit your prejudice,' said du Toit. He withdrew his hand; he also seemed to withdraw into himself. 'I am not sure how I should react to this, Superintendent.' He paused again, as if to begin another battle of silence.

'I've probably misled you,' Roger said hastily. 'If I thought it were political I would probably lean over backwards to try to make sure that my own political leanings wouldn't affect any action I took, or my thinking as a policeman. I didn't admit any prejudice, anyhow; I don't think I have any.'

'If you haven't, you are truly a remarkable man,' said du Toit. He smiled more freely than he had since Roger had entered the office. 'But of course you are remarkable, or I would not be talking to you like this. I should be much more reserved. To answer your question – no, this is not a political matter. The missing person is not connected in politics or in social affairs in any way. In so far as anything which happens in South Africa is assumed to have a political association, it might be regarded as political by some.'

Roger said frowningly: 'I don't quite follow.'

'I mean that if this man were to have disappeared of his own accord, if he were to be found dead, for instance, then there are people in this country and in most of the world who would infer a political reason. It would be nonsense and it would be wrong, but it would be said. Don't misunderstand me,' went on du Toit, raising his hands. 'I know that people do leave South Africa for political reasons, and I think they are mistaken to do so. But I am sure this man did not. He was coming to see an engineering company in England, and might have gone on from here to see another company in the United States. He is a director and substantial stockholder in one of our mining companies, as well as the research director. He also owns one of the very few independent diamond mines in South Africa. Because of these things his work was of importance to South Africa's economy and therefore of interest to the Government, but—' Du Toit paused, then slowly smiled; in that moment he made Roger warm to him as an individual. 'But the Government was as anxious as he and his company for his success.'

Roger said: 'I see.'

'You make that remark seem very profound, Superintendent.'

'I'm not feeling at all profound. If your Government's anxious for the man's success, then there are bound to be people who are anxious for his failure, simply because such a failure would be sure to rub off on the Government. That's too simple to be profound.'

'I think I would disagree with you.' Du Toit stood up. 'But I have no reason at all, no one has any reason at all, to suspect direct political intervention of any kind.' He moved towards Roger, but at the same time looked at one of the panels. 'Much of this wood-carving is done by Bantu craftsmen, Superintendent. You have observed the animals from our game parks, and the historical tableaux of the great treks, but I did not notice you glance towards any of those behind you.' He led the way to the far end of the room, where the carvings were of tall, spindly derricks, of big slag heaps, of mine shafts. Roger studied them as du Toit went on: 'We share a lot of things with Great Britain, problems as well as internal and raw-material situations. It would be very important to you to find oil, wouldn't it?'

Roger looked at him sharply.

'Very.'

'It would be equally important to us.'

'And this missing man was coming to see English manufacturers of machinery which might help you to find oil? Or to bring it up once you found it?'

'Don't jump too quickly to conclusions, please. There is no certainty that oil is the motive – only that it was one of his reasons for coming here. He has many industrial interests. He was coming to discuss arrangements for boring plant, and to arrange terms for engineers and surveyors to go to certain parts of South Africa where we have reason to think there might be oil. Very few people were aware of this. His company tells us that only two other members of the management knew that this was included in his itinerary of the United Kingdom. As far as we can find out no one else apart from the Government was fully aware of his purpose. The police at home are investigating that, but the immediate problem here is to find out what happened to him when he reached London Airport.' Du Toit turned away from the panels, and moved back to the desk, but he did not go to his chair. 'He travelled alone, for secrecy's sake. He was not met at the airport. All his plans were made personally, although we were informed. We expected a call from him yesterday morning, and when it did not come we inquired at the hotel where he had reserved a room. He had not arrived.'

'What hotel?' asked Roger.

'The Georgian, in the Strand.'

'What inquiries did you make at the airport?'

'We simply asked if he—'

'Supposing we start using his name,' suggested Roger.

'Very well, but even that is not as simple as it may sound.

His real name is Van der Lunn. The name under which he was travelling was Lewis.'

'May we use Van der Lunn?'

'If you wish.'

'I think it may help,' said Roger. 'You simply asked if he was on the passenger list, and if all the passengers had been on board the plane – is that it?'

'Yes. They had been.'

'So, presumably, he got off the plane here. Are the details there?' Roger pointed to the files. 'As well as the times of arrival and departure of the plane, and all the relevant information?'

'Yes.'

'Mr du Toit, exactly what do you want me to do? Or the Yard to do? Spell it out for me, will you?'

Where another man might have said, 'You know already,' du Toit moved round his desk, sat down slowly, and began to speak with great deliberation, almost as if he felt that he had to consider each individual word before uttering it. Roger had an impression of a man of high intelligence and great sensitivity; and also the impression of one who had taught himself to pick his way carefully through a bed of thorns.

'I will endeavour to, Superintendent. The Ambassador would be most grateful if you will investigate all the circumstances of the apparent disappearance of Mr Paul Van der Lunn. He would also be grateful if such an investigation could be carried out without attracting public attention. So far as we now know, the Press has no knowledge of the disappearance. We feel it likely that if the knowledge becomes general then such allusions as you yourself have foreseen will be inevitable. If, in your considered view, it will be necessary for Mr Van der Lunn's disappearance to become public knowledge, then we would appreciate it if you will tell us so as much in advance as possible, please.'

Du Toit leaned back as he finished, with his left hand resting lightly on the pale-pink folder. Roger had a feeling that he had only just resisted the impulse to add: 'Have I made myself clear?'

'In your view, what would justify publicity?' inquired Roger.

'We would, of course, bow to your judgement. For our part we would think it necessary if there seemed no other way of tracing Mr Van der Lunn. We would also consider it necessary if you had reason to believe that he had been – injured, or killed.'

Roger flashed: 'Do you seriously think he's been murdered?'

'No. We simply accept the possibility.'

'Had you any reason to believe that he was in danger?'

'None.'

'Let me study the file for half an hour while I'm here,' Roger said. 'It might help me to ask questions of detail, and get us off to a quicker start.' Du Toit handed him the file, and he went on: 'Any corner where I'm on my own will do. I needn't take up your time while I'm looking through the reports.'

Du Toit's rather thin, well-shaped lips curved widely when he smiled.

'You are most considerate,' he said drily. 'There is a smaller room next door.' He led the way to a door on the right, and the nearest of the three secretaries stood up from his desk. 'Mr Hoyt, will you arrange for some tea to be taken to Superintendent West?' He moved across and opened another door, which led on to a small but beautifully-appointed room, more like a study than an office. 'I hope this will be suitable, Superintendent.'

'Perfectly,' Roger said warmly.

He was halfway through a report from a man who signed himself 'J. Jameson' when the door opened on a light tap, and a tall, well-built, immaculate Negro came in, carrying a tea-tray with cake and biscuits. His smile was easy and bright.

'Mr du Toit asked me to tell you, Superintendent, that if you need anything you have only to summon me by pressing the red push-button, or if you wish to speak to him, the green telephone is connected directly with his office. The black one is a line to the Post Office Exchange.'

'That's fine,' Roger said. 'Thanks.'

He watched the door as the other man went out, and began to smile again. Du Toit had not really said a direct word, but he had managed to create exactly the impression that he had wanted; he was busy testing for prejudice. But the reflection soon faded. Roger turned back to the report, reflecting almost ruefully that he would not expect a better one from any of the men at the Yard. The times, the people questioned, the ground covered, even the reactions of individuals, were all here. Yet it told him little more than du Toit had outlined.

Roger spent three-quarters of an hour studying them, then moved the direct-line telephone towards him and dialled the Yard. In a moment he was speaking to Hardy.

Hardy listened ...

'All right,' he said when Roger finished. 'I'll have the men and a car ready so that you can start for the airport as soon as you're back. No need to refer to me; do whatever you think best.'

At least he was in a reasonable mood.

'Thanks,' Roger said. He put that instrument down with one hand and lifted the telephone to du Toit's office with the other. 'May I come in?'

'Of course. I will come for you.' By the time Roger reached the door, it opened and du Toit appeared. The Negro was standing at some filing-cabinets in a corner of the secretaries' office; he didn't look round.

'What I would like is to meet Lieutenant Jameson,' Roger said. 'His reports are particularly lucid. And I'd like him to come with me to London Airport, if that's practical. I might be able to dig out more information there, and Jameson will be able to show me exactly what he did when he was there. Is he available?'

'At once,' du Toit said promptly. He leaned towards his desk and pressed a bell. 'Do you think his reports were comprehensive enough?'

'As far as I can tell, yes,' replied Roger. He heard the door open behind him, but it was not until the newcomer spoke that he realized who it was; even then he did not realize the significance of his presence.

'You rang, sir?' It was the Negro.

'Yes, Lieutenant,' du Toit said. 'Superintendent West wants you to go with him to London Airport, and will require all the assistance you can give him. I think you have already met Lieutenant Jameson, Superintendent. He is an officer in our National Police Force, seconded here for special duties.'

Roger turned round.

Jameson was giving his free, frank smile.

Roger chuckled.

'I won't pretend that didn't catch me bending,' he said, and without thinking held out his hand. As he did so, he had a momentary qualm: was it the thing to do? Jameson quickly dispelled any doubts; there was nothing either timid or hesitant about the way he put out his hand, and his grip was firm.

'I will help in every way I can,' he promised.

'First question,' Roger said. 'Do you know Mr Paul Van der Lunn?'

'Oh yes, sir.'

'And, of course, the lieutenant fully understands the situation, and the dangers of misunderstanding,' du Toit said. 'Thank you for your help, Superintendent.'

'I hope it soon leads to finding Van der Lunn,' Roger said.

3

THE AIRPORT

AS THEY drove towards the tunnel which took the road beneath the runways at the airport, a jet came hurtling out of the skies as if it would skim the very top of the police-car, dark gases pouring from its engines like the angry breath of some giant monster. As they drove along, Roger next to

Jameson at the back, black-haired Chief Inspector Klemm next to the driver – Detective-Sergeant Liss – the plane touched down very gently. Soon it taxied out of sight behind the airport buildings. A dozen other aircraft were on the huge field, and almost as soon as the noise of the first one faded, another took off, roaring as if it were carrying thunder into the heavens.

The Superintendent whom Roger knew best at the airport was on holiday; his second-in-command was Hammerton, a man whom Roger did not know well, but who was reputed to be a good detective with a high conceit of himself. The Airport Police were quite distinct from the Metropolitan Police, but they worked well together, and liaised closely.

The two shook hands, and Hammerton gave a rather sardonic smile.

'Nice to see you, Handsome. Still don't trust us, I see.'

'What have I done?' asked Roger.

Hammerton nodded to Klemm, whose black hair was much too heavily oiled. He had rather thin, sallow features and deepset eyes, which shone as he smiled at Jameson.

'The Yard never believes that anyone else is capable of doing their job properly, do they, Lieutenant?'

'If that is so I have yet to find it out,' replied Jameson.

'Can't afford to sit on the fence too long when you're dealing with the Yard,' said Hammerton. They were in his office, one window of which looked over a part of the airfield. The atmosphere was a little uncanny, because the only sounds in here came from the men. This seemed to make the airfield remote, as if the roaring of aircraft and all other outside sounds were imagined and not real. 'Still looking for Mr Lewis?'

'We are most anxious to find him.'

'Still hush-hush?' Hammerton asked Roger.

'Very.'

'That's a pity.'

'Why?'

'Because the one man who might be able to help us is a newspaperman,' answered Hammerton. 'He was here to meet someone else off the aircraft Lewis arrived on, and believe me he wouldn't miss much. But if you question him he'll put two and two together, and make five out of it in *The Daily Globe*. Such as calling Lewis, Van der Lunn.'

'We might have to resort to the newspaperman,' Roger said. 'Have you done any double-checking?'

'Some.'

'Anything else turned up?'

'Only a few details,' answered Hammerton. 'Van der Lunn was on the flight all right. The crew had two days off and have just come back for another flight to Johannesburg – there's a change in stewards, but that's not unusual. I talked to the second pilot, who keeps his eyes open, and to one of the stewardesses. Quite reliable,' Hammerton added with a glance at Jameson. 'I showed them a photograph and they both say that he was on board. He wasn't well, though.'

'Not well?' asked Jameson. For the first time there was something like eagerness in his voice.

'Didn't eat much, didn't drink much, just kept himself to himself. The plane touched down at Nairobi and Cairo, but he didn't get off for the usual walk round the airfield. I can tell you another thing,' Hammerton went on, with obvious satisfaction. 'I've checked with Customs, and they recognized him – he had one suitcase and one briefcase, with overnight things in one, and some engineering journals and papers in the other. They didn't search, just glanced at them casually. He didn't seem well, and a porter led him off. The porter took him to the lounge, and left him. We haven't been able to trace him since. We might if we asked the taxi-drivers, the porters, and all the rest of the *hoi polloi*, but something would be bound to leak about his identity.'

'You aren't sure whether he went off by taxi, or private car, or by the air terminal bus?' Roger said.

'Not the bus. I was able to check with one of the stewardesses – she travelled on it, too.'

'This is at once disappointing and yet most thorough,' Jameson observed. He was looking hard at Hammerton. 'I am very grateful.'

'Can't leave things undone so that the Yard can come and

tell us how to do our job,' Hammerton said drily. 'Care to see the crew while they're here, Handsome?'

'What time do they take off?'

'Seven o'clock.'

'Then we've a couple of hours,' Roger said. 'I'd like to do one or two other things first. That porter—'

'He's gone – but he knows nothing more. He was too anxious to get another job.'

'What are the chances of finding the taxi-drivers who were here when the plane came in?'

'We'll spread the word and try to find out. They'll contact us if they're regulars, but if they just brought someone in from the Big Smoke they would only wait long enough to pick up a fare going back. The only way to trace them then would be a general request through newspapers or television. That would bring the reporters on us like a pack of hounds, but you know that, don't you?'

'Yes,' said Roger. 'May I use your phone?'

'Help yourself,' Hammerton waved a big hand towards the instrument on his desk. The operator answered almost at once.

'Get me the editorial department of *The Globe* newspaper, will you?' He held on, aware of Hammerton's almost comically-startled expression. Then another telephone bell rang. Hammerton answered it, and Roger heard him say:

'Can't it wait?' There was a pause before the airport man went on ungraciously: 'Oh, all right, I'll come.' He put the receiver down heavily, and spoke to Klemm. 'Some trouble over a packet of industrial diamonds. Customs wants me. Sorry.' He nodded to Roger and Jameson and went out. As the door closed, a man said: 'Editorial,' into Roger's left ear, and Jameson spoke quite urgently into his right. 'Excuse me, Superintendent.'

'This is Superintendent West of New Scotland Yard,' Roger said into the telephone. 'Ask Mr Soames or his deputy to speak to me urgently, please.' He covered the mouthpiece with his hand and looked up at the South African. 'What was that?'

'If it was Mr Van der Lunn on that aircraft, sir, he was behaving in a most unusual manner.'

'Why?'

'Mr Van der Lunn does not like staying in aeroplanes if he can avoid it. He is a restless passenger, and whenever he has a chance to leave the aircraft, he does so. I would not like to be sure it was Mr Van der Lunn.'

'Nice point,' Roger said. He heard the newspaperman's voice, and added quickly: 'Check with Klemm, will you? Keep it under our hats for the time being ... Mr Soames? ... I'm fine, thanks, but with a bit of a problem on my hands ... Yes, I would feel funny without one, wouldn't I?' he laughed mechanically, thinking of Jameson's doubts about the identity of the man on the aircraft. 'As a matter of fact one of your men might be able to help us, and I'd like to get in touch with him.'

He knew that Soames was a kind of one-man-band at *The Globe*, one of the old type of Fleet Street editor whose chief fault was reluctance to delegate any real authority; but he was known to have the fierce loyalty of his staff.

'Who d'you want?' he asked.

'Nightingale.'

The silence which followed surprised Roger, for Soames was not one to hesitate. The delay went on for so long that Roger wondered if they had been cut off. The other two were whispering together by the window, Klemm's black glossy hair gleaming in the light, Jameson's a mass of small, tight curls, reflecting nothing.

'What do you know about Nightingale?' demanded Soames, abruptly.

'I'm asking you where he is.'

'Don't you know?'

Roger was tempted to ask the editor to stop stalling, then realized that there must be a strong reason for his attitude, so he answered mildly:

'No, I don't. He was at London Airport on Monday afternoon, and I'm looking for a man who came off a plane and hasn't been heard of since. I thought Nightingale might be able to help; he keeps his eyes open.'

'He hasn't been heard of since,' Soames echoed.

'That's right.'

'I mean Nightingale.'

'Nightingale what?'

'Hasn't been heard of since.' Soames sounded very gruff.

This time it was Roger's turn to be reduced to silence. Although he understood what the other man had said, it was almost impossible to credit it. He shifted his position so that he could squat on the corner of the desk, and asked:

'Do you mean he really hasn't been seen and hasn't reported since he came to the airport?'

'That's what I mean.'

'And you don't know where he is?'

'I don't. West, what makes you want to talk to him?' Now there was an anxious note in the editor's voice. 'Don't give me that stuff about wondering if he happened to notice anything.'

'How long are you going to be at your office?' asked Roger.

'Until after midnight.'

'May I come and talk about this?'

'Whenever you like.'

'If Nightingale shows up, send a message to the Yard, will you?'

'Yes. Can't you give me a clue?'

'I've a missing man to find, and so have you. I didn't know of any connection before and I don't now, but obviously there could be. What job was Nightingale covering?'

'Diamond smuggling,' answered *The Globe* editor promptly. 'I don't know whether you've been told about it, but a lot of industrial diamonds are being smuggled out of South Africa. They're sold to big users in various countries, at cut prices – and a lot of them are then stolen from the buyers, who can't do much about it because they've bought diamonds they know have been stolen. Did you know about this?'

'I knew some had been stolen in New York and Amsterdam,' said Roger. 'We've been asked to keep our eyes open.' He had little doubt that Hammerton was on that investigation now. 'How many countries are involved to your knowledge?'

'Seven.'

Roger hoped that he showed no sign of the shock that total gave him; in fact, the Yard knew very little about this racket.

'Wheels within wheels,' Soames went on. 'Nightingale has been on the story for several weeks. Is that what your man was involved in?'

'Not as far as I know,' Roger said. 'I'll come straight up to your office.'

'Don't let anyone see you or I'll have half my staff trying to sell me a story of crime inside *The Globe*,' said Soames. He rang off.

Jameson and Klemm had finished talking, so Roger had to push this new development to the back of his mind, and consider Jameson's theory, that the man at the airport had not been Van der Lunn. At least Hammerton wasn't back yet. He had been called out by Customs officers about industrial diamonds, and that seemed too much for coincidence. Why did one always think of South Africa when thinking of diamonds? He mustn't forget that Soames didn't. *Seven* countries. He watched the alert face of the African and the sallow face of Klemm. There was something in common between them, a kind of restrained eagerness.

'Let's have it,' Roger said.

'Everything I know about Mr Van der Lunn contradicts what we have been told about the passenger,' insisted Jameson. 'I think it is certain that if it was Mr Van der Lunn, then he was sick. Inspector Klemm thinks perhaps it would be a good idea if we were to question the crew of the aircraft and show them a better photograph of Mr Van der Lunn. We are not likely to be able to interview them again for some days.'

'Unless you'd like to do it yourself now,' Klemm said.

'Jameson knows a lot more about it than I do. Have a go at them,' Roger agreed. 'Don't forget that one of them might have seen the passenger get off – the fact that the

26

stewardess and the second pilot didn't, doesn't mean a thing. Klemm, you know Nightingale of *The Globe*, don't you?'

'I know what a long nose he's got.'

'He's missing, too,' said Roger. 'And since the night that Mr Van der Lunn was last seen. Thread him into the questions – the crew probably knew him. He was chasing a story on stolen and smuggled industrial diamonds – any possibility that Van der Lunn might know anything about such diamonds, Lieutenant?'

'He would know something, yes. He is a director of de Beers, and he also owns a small mine which he inherited from his father. It is an independent-producing mine, but sells only to de Beers, the diamond monopoly. Also he surveys for blue dirt as well as all kinds of minerals such as oil, uranium, gold, platinum, and copper. He would not smuggle or deal in stolen diamonds. He is a very wealthy man, but ...' Jameson broke off. 'It is very interesting indeed, Superintendent.'

'When you're sure you've done all you can here, get back to the Yard,' Roger said. 'Don't report to South Africa House until we've been able to talk things over.' He gave the lieutenant a reassuring smile as he went towards the door. As he reached it, it opened and Hammerton came in, obviously not pleased.

'Found anything?' Roger asked.

'Sand where there should have been diamonds – can't do very much with a man who's got two small wash-leather bags full of sand rolled up in his pyjamas and a pair of socks, though, can you?' Seeing Roger's expression, he added hastily: 'Don't worry, we know the chap, and I'm having him followed. Queer thing, though.'

'What is?'

'We get a lot of whispers about diamonds being brought into the country, but never find any. We've had a lot of near misses like this one. You know we're on the lookout for packets being smuggled from New York and Amsterdam, don't you?'

'Yes.' *And* five other countries, thought Roger.

'Where are you off to?' asked Hammerton.

'I'm going back to town,' Roger answered. 'Jameson and Klemm are going to talk to the crew, and there's a job you can do for me if you will.'

'What is it?'

'Let me know all you can about a *Globe* reporter named Nightingale,' Roger said. 'How often he's been here, who he talks to, whether he meets any special planes, anything you can dig up – including whether he has any colleagues working on the airfield with him. Think you might have some word for me by eight o'clock tonight?'

'I'll try to,' said Hammerton. 'I never did like Nightingale. I hope he's got himself into trouble.'

Roger was very thoughtful on his way back to the Yard. Butterworth, the Detective-Superintendent who knew more about the ways of diamond thieves than anyone else in the Yard, was out on a job, but a Chief Inspector who often worked with him reported that no official requests for help over diamonds had been made except from New York and Amsterdam.

'Industrial and small diamonds are known to have been stolen in small parcels from Paris, Bangkok, West Berlin, and Madrid, though. We haven't been asked for help.'

So the Yard did know more than he, Roger, had realized; that was cheering.

Roger left for Fleet Street almost at once.

4

THE EDITOR DECIDES

THE STRAND, with the Law Courts towering on the left, stretched almost empty of cars towards Fleet Street, where the road narrowed and the buildings on either side became massive and modern giants towering over the midgets of the past. Newspaper headlines and newspaper names seemed to be on every hoarding and every window. Six huge red buses in a row came tearing down from Ludgate Circus as Roger's car swung to cross the road; the driver was going to do a U-turn. 'Police-cars can do anything,' the cynics would complain, but this wasn't marked as a police-car. The driver pulled skilfully behind the end bus and stopped almost directly outside the office of *The Globe*. A pale-faced policeman came strolling along, as if he had all the time in the world, the words: 'May I see your licence?' on his lips. The driver got out, winked at him, and opened the door for Roger. The policeman began to stare thoughtfully across the road.

The Globe was not only London's oldest daily newspaper, it was housed in London's oldest newspaper building, a Victorian relic of which a lot of people were proud and about which a few were sentimental. Inside was a panelled hall, scratched and worn, leading to passages, lifts, small boys waiting to run errands, old commissionaires who looked as if they were waiting to die. Roger slipped into an open grille lift which was about to close; the lift-man nodded, as if he were weary of going up and down, up and down. A small, greasy-haired boy with some envelopes and a middle-aged woman with dyed red hair and too much make-up both got out on the floor marked *Advertisements*.

'Editorial, please,' Roger said.

Editorial was a maze of passages created by wooden partitions which hid most of the workers from sight, but did not keep out the noise. Typewriters clattered with urgent speed, teletype machines ticked their gossip, a dozen telephone bells seemed to be ringing on a muted note, dozens of people were talking at the same time. One man kept saying:

'Speak up, can't hear you ... Speak up ... Speak up!'

All this noise floated over the tops of the partition walls, but at the far end of a passage some offices were completely walled off. One of the doors was marked: *Editor*. Roger went in. An unexpected beauty of a girl, charming as a Mayfair model, elegant but not sleek, with a smile which was bright but not forced or brazen, looked up at him from a desk.

'Mr West?'

'Yes.'

'Mr Soames would like you to go in at once,' she said. She stood up from her desk, which was quite large and tidy, although there were a lot of papers on it, including copies of the evening's newspapers and some of that very morning's. She went to a communicating door, and it would have been impossible not to notice her legs, beautiful legs, and the way her dress gave subtle emphasis to her figure. She opened the door, called 'Mr West' to an unseen occupant, and stood aside for Roger to enter. They had to pass very closely, and their bodies touched. Roger did not recognize the perfume which she used, but it had a rare, almost heady quality.

Soames was at his huge square desk, a mountain of a desk on which newspapers, letters, proofs, and oddments of copy-paper made the snow on the peaks, and the ink-stands, ash-trays, telephones, bottles, glasses, tea-pot, milk-jug, and cups made the foothills. He half-rose from a big old-fashioned swivel-chair, a rugged and chunky man in his sixties, with a lot of grizzled hair and a stubble of yesterday's beard in the deep crevices of his face. He had shaggy eyebrows and the deepest of deep blue, penetrating eyes.

He stretched out his hands, gripped, and dropped back in-to his chair.

'Not a day older,' he almost jeered. 'Still the Yard's glamour boy, I see.'

'Still the same peculiar sense of humour,' Roger retorted, sitting on a chair placed comfortably for him. The girl had gone out. 'What's this about Nightingale?'

'And still on the ball. Who's going to give first – you or me?'

'Off the record?' asked Roger.

'Must it be?'

'Absolutely, for the time being.'

'I'm not going to like that,' complained Soames.

'Then let's just talk about Nightingale,' Roger said. 'He was after smugglers of industrial diamonds, expected to find someone on that plane, presumably went after them, and didn't come back. So he could be still on the trail or he could have met with an accident.'

'Right,' Soames confirmed. 'You win. Off the record, what's going on?'

'Do you know a man named Paul Van der Lunn?' asked Roger.

Soames shifted back in his chair, and seemed to settle into it as awkwardly as a huge piece of granite. He had a prominent jaw, which jutted just now. He gripped the padded arms of his chair and his fingers began to knead the worn red leather.

'The director of the Afra Mining Company?'

'Yes.'

'So it *was* him,' said Soames. He breathed out through his nostrils, as if trying to pretend that he was some dragon whose belly was filled with fire and brimstone. 'I should never have agreed to keeping this off the record. Nightingale telephoned from the airport – that was the last thing we heard of him. He said he thought Van der Lunn was on the plane, but couldn't be sure. He went after someone else, and I checked to find out if Van der Lunn was in town. We asked South Africa House, asked the London office of the Afra Mining Company, and asked the news agencies who had been at London Airport. Each time the answer was the same : No. But it *was* him.'

'Wasn't Nightingale positive enough?'

'Nothing is sure enough for us except absolute proof.'

'Did Nightingale speak to you about Van der Lunn?'

'Yes.'

'Do I have to use a hammer and chisel to get the story out of you?' demanded Roger.

'You could try telling me why you're interested.'

'All right,' said Roger, promptly. 'Van der Lunn was travelling under an assumed name – Lewis. He started out on the plane from Johannesburg as far as we can tell, and was supposed to have disembarked at London Airport. He wasn't seen afterwards. We've checked closely, and there's some doubt as to whether it was Van der Lunn. He didn't behave like himself, and, if it was him, then he was either ill or

31

frightened – we don't know which.' Roger paused. But as Soames simply waited, those deep, deep-set eyes unwinking, he went on. 'South Africa House made preliminary inquiries, got nowhere, and called us in. The job was handed to me by Hardy from the Commissioner, and I was ordered to make sure that it was kept secret. Do you know du Toit of South Africa House?'

'Slightly.'

'What's his reputation?'

'He's okay.'

'He convinced me that there are good reasons for secrecy so (a) I'm under Home Office orders to say nothing, and (b) I'm sure that it's right to say nothing.'

'So don't let me do anything to make you change your mind,' retorted Soames drily. After a long pause, he went on: 'You were going to ask me something.'

Roger thought back, and at the same time reflected how much he liked this man, that Soames's reputation was at least as good as du Toit's, and that Soames's political convictions as well as the editorial slant of his newspaper were anti-South African, or perhaps, more accurately, anti-Apartheid.

'I was going to ask what Nightingale said about Van der Lunn and also what else he said.'

'He told me that he thought this passenger was Van der Lunn,' declared Soames. 'He also said that he stood by at Customs and learned that Van der Lunn was travelling with a passport in the name of Lewis. That this made it seem even more likely that there was a story in it for us. Did I want him to follow his nose and go after Van der Lunn, or did I want him to stay with the industrial diamonds job? He knew that I would always like to get in first on anything which might have a political slant on Anglo-South African relationship, so he gave me the chance. But he really wanted to find the truth about those diamonds. He's been on that particular job for over six months, and it's become almost an obsession with him. A lot of parcels of diamonds, mostly industrial or for costume pieces and bought illegally, are being stolen from many parts of the world. From South Africa, Amsterdam, New York—'

'I know,' Roger interjected.

'So you should. Well, Nightingale must crack it, to prove he's the man he thinks he is. I left him to find his diamond smuggler, while I put another man on to the Van der Lunn story. I took this chap off next morning because there was no lead. I can let you see his notes, if you like.'

'I'd like to see them very much,' Roger said.

Soames leaned forward, shifted some proofs and a newspaper from a heap, and disclosed an old-fashioned inter-office speaking-box. He flicked up a lever.

'Yes, Mr Soames?' said the girl in the outer office.

'Got those notes from Bennett?'

'Yes.'

'Good girl. Bring 'em in.'

'Yes. Mr Soames—'

'Well?'

'You said you did not want to be interrupted, but Mr Ossenden has been trying to get you. I said you were out of the office, but would call him the moment you got back.'

'Oh, did you.' Soames seemed to glower. 'Get him for me, and put him through into the board-room, I'll take the call there. Bring those notes in to Mr West here and give him any help he needs, especially the background on Nightingale's disappearance. Nothing in from Nightingale, is there?'

'Nothing at all.'

Soames grunted, flicked the lever down, pushed his chair back, and glowered at the wall above Roger's head. Ossenden was the chairman of *The Globe*'s directors, the only man who could tell Soames what to do, and it seemed obvious that one of the periodic clashes between the two men was reaching a climax. Soames stared down at Roger, but was hardly aware of him. He gripped the arms of the chair more tightly, and stood up. Only then was the truth about this big and powerful man revealed; he was crippled by osteo-arthritis, and could not stand upright. He had to lean against the desk as he moved, and with an almost savage gesture he snatched at a heavy walking-stick hooked on to a knob at the back of his chair.

'Why can't I come back in five minutes?' Roger asked, and wondered whether Soames's fierce pride would make him resent reference to his infirmity.

Soames flashed a grin which bared his big, slightly-discoloured teeth and a gleam or two of gold fillings.

'Because what I have to say must not be heard out there, and I'm not used to keeping my voice down when I want to speak my mind.' He stumped off, using a small door in a corner away from the door to the secretary's office, thrust it back with the ferrule of his stick and pushed again as it swung into him before he had got through. It closed behind him. Roger could hear the thump of the stick, and for those few seconds thought only of the editor, and his brave spirit and his infirmity. Then he moved to his chair and sat down, thinking over everything that had been said, and the coincidental thread of the industrial diamonds.

Was that simply conscience?

There was a tap at the door and the girl came in, carrying some manila folders. She had a grace of movement which matched the rest of her. Her hair was on the dark side of gold, waved but not curly; just right. She had honey-coloured eyes, and Roger realized that it was their colour which made her so unusual.

Roger asked: 'Is the arthritis getting any worse?'

'Yes,' she answered. 'It's agony for him to move. It hurts to see him, doesn't it?'

'When I first knew him, he played cricket as well as tennis and soccer.'

'So he did when I first knew him,' the girl replied. She smiled at Roger's surprised expression. 'Yes, I've known him all my life. He's my uncle. I call him Mr Soames because we decided that it was the best thing to do in the office. Everybody here knows the relationship, of course, but we don't have to throw it in their faces.'

'I suppose not,' said Roger drily. He drew a deep breath. 'Let me have a look at those notes, will you?'

The girl opened the folder out on the desk in front of him. He continued to sit while she stood close to him; very close to him. He did not actually wish that she wouldn't, but he was a little too aware of her, unable to concentrate as much as he knew he should. She pointed to one or two notes written in a sprawling hand; her fingers were long and shapely, and she used natural varnish on nicely-shaped nails.

'You see, Bennett telephoned all the usual places. Then he went to South Africa House – he saw a detective named Jameson – and afterwards to the hotel where "Lewis" had booked in, but there was no trace of him. He went to the offices of the Afra Mining Company at a quarter past eleven that morning – Tuesday. They simply said that Mr Van der Lunn hadn't arrived and they assumed he had been delayed in South Africa.' The girl had a way of talking that was curiously like Soames's – direct, economical, straight to the point. 'Here are the notes made of Mr Bennett's conversation with Mr Soames, too.'

Roger scanned through these; they added nothing to what Soames had told him.

'May I have copies?' he asked.

The girl selected a large envelope from the file.

'Mr Soames thought you might like photostat copies, so they're all in here.'

Roger laughed. 'Thanks.' He opened the envelope and glanced through the contents, mechanically checking that everything was there. 'How freely may you talk?'

She had moved away a little; not far, but noticeably. She looked down on him, smiling, almost laughing. At him? He wondered how old she was. Older than he had first thought, probably in her late twenties, although she might be only twenty-four or five. She was rather slender-bosomed, and yet the pale-brown dress with its piping of dark green was most provocatively cut.

'I shall know where to stop,' she assured him. 'I really am my uncle's niece! What would you like to know?'

'What success did Nightingale have on the diamond-smuggling job?' asked Roger. 'Did he suspect anyone? Had he any contacts in the ring? That kind of thing.'

'Why do you want to know?'

'If he looked like cracking the ring, then it's conceivable the ring found a way to stop him.'

'Do you know Nightingale?' inquired the girl.

'Slightly.'

'Then you may not know him well enough to be sure that only one thing would stop him, Mr West. Either he's still working on the investigation or he's dead – or at least incapacitated.' She spoke as if there could be no possibility of doubt. 'But surely you're more interested in Bennett's report about the man who called himself Lewis.' When Roger didn't answer, she went on: 'You don't seriously think that the two cases might be connected, do you?'

Before Roger could answer, thudding sounds came from the next room. As the girl drew back from him, the inner door was thrust open, and Soames appeared, wielding his thick walking-stick like a rapier, to keep the door back. He was grinning, obviously with satisfaction

'Faith, go along and tell Comp we'll run the first leader. He can scrap the other piece of nonsense.' Soames moved to his chair, hooked the stick behind, and supported himself on his powerful arms until he could drop into it. He grunted; the sound was almost a wince. He looked up at Roger tight-lipped, but apart from pain there was the fiery glint of triumph in his eyes. 'Did Faith give you everything you asked for?'

'Yes,' said Roger. 'But she didn't tell me everything I wanted to know – whether Nightingale thought he was close to the truth about the smuggling, for instance. Was he?'

'He certainly thought so.'

'Won't you be more specific?' Roger asked.

After a long pause, Soames shifted forward until he rested his thick forearms on the desk; muscles bulged inside the sleeves of his jacket.

'I'd like to make a condition, and ask for the first chance of the Van der Lunn story when you can release it, but I'll leave that to your natural sense of justice.' There was a derisive note in his voice. 'Yes, he thought he was near the end of the hunt. He believed that the ring-leader of a powerful smuggling organization was on Monday's plane. Whether he was right or wrong we shan't know until he reports.'

Roger said: 'If he reports. Talking of reporting . . .'

'Yes?'

'When are you going to report him missing?'

'Meaning, do we want you to look for him?'

'Yes.'

Soames hesitated, and then the fierce grin flashed again. This time he seemed to be even more amused than he had before, as if this was a great joke.

'We'll report him missing any time you'll agree to treat it as secret.'

Roger chuckled.

'As from now,' he promised. He stood up, leaned across the desk to shake hands, and went on: 'If you hear anything from or about Nightingale you'll let me know at once, won't you?'

'Yes.'

'Thanks. And how about letting me have photostat copies of the reports on his case, too?'

'The copies are in a thick envelope on Faith's desk. She'll give them to you as you go out.' Again there was that quick, powerful handshake. 'Let me know if you find Van der Lunn, won't you?'

5

THE SEARCH

ROGER TURNED into his office at New Scotland Yard just before seven o'clock, took off his jacket and hung it on a peg of the hat-stand, lifted his telephone and said: 'Get my wife, will you?' rang off and rounded the desk and opened the files. He had already studied them in the car on the way from Fleet Street, and knew most of the information off by heart; he was checking how much he still had to impress on his memory. He was halfway through when his telephone bell rang. He stretched out for it, and said:

'Guess who this is?'

'West, I hope,' said the Assistant Commissioner.

Roger nearly dropped the telephone, hardly knowing whether to laugh or to be extra cautious; it was usual for the operator to put him straight through to Janet, his wife.

'West,' Roger confirmed.

'How far have you got with the Van der Lunn investigation?'

'I've just come up from *Information*. A picture of Van der Lunn, who seems to have been travelling under a false passport, in the name of Paul Lewis, is going out to all London Divisions and other police forces tonight, for spot checking,' Roger said. 'We want to make sure that his body hasn't been found and isn't in some morgue. I've been to London Airport, and unless Klemm or Jameson—'

'Jameson?'

'A man seconded to the job from South Africa House.'

'That's all right.'

'Unless they've discovered something, and there's no report on my desk, I don't know any more about what happened to Van der Lunn than I did when I started. I do know that there's some doubt as to whether it was really Van der Lunn. There's even some doubt whether he really left South Africa. If it was him, then he was either ill or feigning, or else under some kind of pressure.'

'How did you get on at South Africa House?'

'As well as they hoped, I think.'

Hardy actually chuckled.

'Stay with this job all the time,' he said. 'Tell Janet that you won't know what home is like for the next few days.'

Janet would probably say that would be nothing new, but this wasn't the moment to find out whether Hardy would think that funny. Roger rang off, pencilled a note, and heard footsteps in the passage. As they drew nearer the door, his telephone bell rang again. This time he was more cautious.

'West speaking.'

'Very formal tonight, Mr West, aren't you?' This was Janet; and Janet nearly always made him feel good. As he sat back, he had a momentary glimpse of Soames's niece, Faith, but it was gone in a flash, and he hardly noticed it.

'Hallo, darling,' Janet went on. 'I know what you're going to tell me. You're going to be late.'

'Late-ish, anyhow,' Roger said. 'What kind of day has it been?'

'When you start asking that kind of question you're going to be very late,' said Janet resignedly. 'Just average, dear – Martin's up in his room with a fellow art student, female, talking earnestly about abstracts and modernism and all the rest. Richard telephoned to say he'll be late too, and not to get any supper ready for him.'

'Girl-friend?' inquired Roger.

'I shouldn't think so, but he may be fooling me.'

'Now would any of your family do that?' asked Roger. There was a tap at the door, but he didn't answer. 'Sweet, I must go. I'll make it just as soon as I can, but I might possibly be called out of London. Don't be too surprised if I am.'

'From this moment on, I'm expecting it,' Janet declared. 'I can't expect to have lunch *and* sleep with you on the same day, can I? Roger!'

'Now what?'

'Did you know you were going to be out tonight? Is that why you took me to lunch?'

'It would have been a good idea, but I didn't even give it a thought,' Roger said. 'When I get round to practising small deceits on you, I'll warn you in advance. Jan, I've two chaps almost breaking the door down. I must go. See you.' He rang off, and paused, and reflected, and then called: 'Come in.' As the door opened he was thinking of Janet, and the fact that he seemed to be making these calls more and more often; that he was getting home later and later more often, too.

First Klemm and then Jameson came in, and as the reflections passed, Roger slid back to the Van der Lunn problem almost without thinking. He waved to chairs, and they sat down; it was obvious from their expressions that they had no good news to report. Klemm looked hot and rather dejected, like a dishevelled and out-of-temper Spaniard. Jameson was fresh and as immaculate as he had been in the office.

'Nothing,' Klemm said.

'I've got a lot of inquiries going out now,' said Roger. 'We may hear something during the night or tomorrow morning. Meanwhile ...' He told them the story of Nightingale's disappearance, and what Nightingale had been doing, watching Jameson all the time he spoke. Jameson had a gift for showing no expression, but there was a look about him, a tension at his lips, which suggested to Roger that he was probably holding his thoughts on leash.

Now, Roger said: 'How much do you know about this diamond stealing, Lieutenant?'

'I know it has been going on,' answered Jameson. 'It is not uncommon, you understand. Many parcels of diamonds which are consigned quite legally from Kimberley to the world's capitals are intercepted and stolen. That is always a matter for the national police to handle. We have reason to believe that smuggling diamonds out of the Union is on the increase. We at South Africa House have not been asked to act, although we have been informed. We hear indirectly that diamonds so smuggled are sold overseas, and often stolen back from the purchasers! Perhaps a kind of rough justice.' When Roger didn't comment, Jameson went on: 'Are you suggesting, sir, that these matters could be connected with Mr Van der Lunn's disappearance?'

'Yes, obviously.'

'To suspect Mr Van der Lunn of any part in smuggling is quite impossible,' Jameson said. 'But—'

'Is it really?' Roger interrupted.

'I find it so.'

'How often does he come to London?'

Jameson answered very slowly in that rather husky and attractive voice: 'Perhaps once in three months, perhaps a little more often at certain times. He has so many business interests. But Mr West—' He broke off.

'I've a file from *The Globe* here giving all of Nightingale's findings and his opinions about the diamond troubles,' Roger said. 'And we've been working on the case – here's our file, as well as a copy of the file the airport police have kept. Will you go through these, check the dates when diamonds consigned to English firms have failed to reach their destination, and when they have actually been found on passengers or aircraft. Then check with the dates on which Mr Van der Lunn has come to London?'

After a long pause, Jameson said: 'Yes, sir.'

'Is this my job, too?' asked Klemm, almost gloomily.

'Yes.'

'Mind if I take an hour off first, sir? I can slip over and see my wife and the nippers,' said Klemm. He lived in Lambeth, across the Thames.

'An hour won't make any difference,' Roger agreed. 'Can you use an hour, Lieutenant?'

Jameson said: 'I have no one expecting me, sir. If I could have the use of a desk somewhere, and these reports, I could begin the comparison.'

'Fix a desk,' Roger said to Klemm.

The two men went out, taking the files, Jameson still looking doubtful; perhaps it would be more true to say that he was looking worried. Roger pulled a pad towards him and jotted down notes of what he had already done, and what he thought now needed doing. He spent longer at this than he expected. He double-checked everything he had discovered at Soames's office, and kept thinking about the possibility that Nightingale had been murdered. There was the 'coincidence' of the two disappearances, too; it was almost impossible for him to believe that. It was curious that Jameson had been so emphatic about Van der Lunn being above suspicion, equally curious that he had not mentioned an obvious possibility – that Van der Lunn might have been kidnapped because of something he had discovered about the traffic in diamonds.

When Klemm and Jameson had finished the analysis, there should be a much clearer picture of the case, and they should be through by half past nine or ten, which gave Roger a couple of hours.

He knew what he ought to do: telephone for a car and a driver and go home – to Chelsea, ten minutes drive away, and spend an hour there. Janet would be happy to get supper for him, and he would be able to relax at home much better than he could here. Then he faced a fact which in its way

41

was unpalatable: he was losing the ability to relax anywhere. That tied up with his objection to the way Gorlay had talked, and later to Hardy's manner. He was too tense. He did not know of any special reason for it, but there must be one. It was worth looking for. He felt compelled to stay close to his desk in case reports arrived, and yet he knew that such reports would reach him almost as quickly if he were home.

He tried to convince himself that a kind of sixth sense was working in him, and that he knew he ought to stay at the Yard, but emotionally he rejected this.

He looked through the reports in his briefcase, the ones which had been on his desk, and tried to convince himself that these must be dealt with tonight. As he looked through them, he admitted to himself that all could have waited.

He could go across to the pub in Cannon Row, and get dinner or a snack, but it would mean talking and drinking with others from the Yard, and he did not feel like it. He sent for a messenger to get him coffee and sandwiches, and was waiting for the elderly constable to come back with these, when his telephone bell rang.

'Mr Pendleton of South-West Division would like a word with you,' said the operator.

Pendleton was an old acquaintance, one who would not ring through as late as this for the sake of a chat.

'Put him through,' Roger said.

A moment later, the Divisional Superintendent spoke in a voice which had a slightly north-country inflection.

'Hallo, Handsome. I think I might have some news for you.' Somehow Roger almost expected him to say 'for thee'. 'I've just had the circular and the photograph of the man Lewis. I think I can tell you where he is.'

6

RAID

DARKNESS WAS settling gauntly over London as the police moved on the hotel where the missing man might be. It was just after eight o'clock. Roger was in the Divisional Superintendent's car, being driven by a middle-aged officer who seemed to drive by instinct, knowing every corner, every twist in the long main road, every traffic light, and divining the intention of other drivers. Three more police-cars were converging on the hotel, which faced Clapham Common, a broad stretch of parkland on the far side of the river from Roger's home yet within a stone's throw of it. As the car turned into the road which overlooked the common, a couple showed up in the headlights, squirming on the grass beneath a tree, oblivious of the rest of the world, or else not caring.

'One of these days we're going to have to clean up the parks,' Pendleton remarked sourly.

'How far away is this place?' asked Roger.

'The man with the one-track mind. Just round the next corner,' Pendleton answered. 'Queer thing, coincidence. If our regular police-surgeon hadn't been on holiday, we wouldn't have used Dr Abbott. If we hadn't used Abbott we wouldn't have recognized this chap when he went to see him as a patient.' Roger had already heard the story, once, but Pendleton was always inclined to be garrulous, partly to make sure that he rammed his point right home. 'And if Abbott hadn't come round to the station tonight and seen the photograph, we'd still be in the dark. Funny thing, coincidence,' he added prosily.

There were stranger ones . . .

A board was fastened to the wall surrounding a corner house, reading: *Common View Hotel*; that was the place.

The stone wall was high and looked thick. Shrubs and trees showed behind it, hiding much of the hotel building itself, but Roger could see a grey slate roof, the chimneys, the top windows. There were two drive gates, and a small circular drive with a shrubbery in the middle. This house was like hundreds which faced parks and commons in the London area. A light shone at the porch, and as the car moved slowly past a light was switched on over the name-board, showing it up very brightly. A youth on a bicycle came out, whistling. A second police-car passed, coming from the other direction; Jameson and Klemm were in this, Klemm driving. The raid had been laid on by Pendleton, and Roger resisted a temptation to ask questions; the Superintendent would get round to everything in good time.

Three houses along there was a narrow road, and another police-car was parked in it.

'That's covering the back. We've got one on the far corner, and the one with the coloured chap will wait across the road near the common,' Pendleton explained. 'Not exactly expecting trouble, are you?'

'I don't know what to expect.'

'Well, we're ready for anything,' Pendleton said confidently. 'We'll go in now. Okay?'

'Yes.'

'Impatient so-and-so,' said Pendleton. They were back on the road overlooking the common, and turned into the hotel driveway. Lights showed upstairs and downstairs. A man sat reading an evening paper close to a window with a standard lamp by his chair, and the scene of a small private hotel could hardly have been more normal. Yet the place had a dilapidated look. As the car pulled up just past the front door, Roger saw an old garden umbrella and a child's push-chair in the porch. He got out one side, Pendleton the other, and they entered the wide porch together. Insects were humming and darting about the lamp's cheap, tinny shade. As they opened the door, a bell clanged loudly, obviously in warning to whoever was in charge. The hall was wide, there was an old-fashioned hat-and-coat stand, a shabby imitation Persian carpet, doors which needed repainting, walls which had been distempered a long time ago. A flight of stairs led off to the right, a narrow passage to the left and a door marked *'Private'*.

Nothing happened.

Pendleton looked round and saw a handbell; he picked it up and rang it heartily, and the resulting noise was deafening. As it faded, Roger thought he heard a thump upstairs. Already a warning was flashing in his mind, but Pendleton seemed to take all this for granted.

No one appeared.

'Time we took a look round,' Roger said.

'Okay, okay,' Pendleton agreed.

He broke off when the door marked *'Private'* opened and a tall, lean man appeared, with a kitchen apron round his waist. He had a scared, bird-like look, which may have been partly due to the thick lenses of his glasses. At the same time, a woman appeared on the stairs, youngish, plumpish, with very full calves and very slim ankles. Her dark hair was a frizzy mop against the light on the half-landing above her.

'Good evening,' said the man.

'Can I help you?' asked the woman.

Roger had an impression that she was scared, too, and he was quite sure of one thing: she was breathing hard, as if she had been hurrying. Obviously, there might be a dozen innocent reasons. He spoke to her, as Pendleton spoke to the man.

'We are police-officers.'

'Police!' the man gasped.

'Police,' whispered the woman.

'I believe you have a Mr Lewis staying here,' said Pendleton. 'We'd like to see him, please.'

'Lewis?'

'No one named Lewis is here.'

'No one,' echoed the man.

'You've made a mistake,' declared the woman.

She was almost gasping for breath, and could not prevent herself from glancing upwards when there was another thud on the ceiling. Roger no longer doubted that someone up there was in a hurry. The man with the thick glasses was stretching out one hand, as if to detain Pendleton. The woman said:

'I really don't know what—'

Roger pushed past her and ran up the stairs. As he reached the half-landing he saw the back of a man who was standing in a doorway, and called out to him: 'Stop there!' The man moved farther into the room clumsily, and back-kicked the door. It swung to, in Roger's face. He twisted round and put his shoulder to it, and took the impact without any pain. Someone was leaning or pressing against the other side. He shouted down to Pendleton: 'Watch all the windows!' One or two people were trying to close the door on him, but he had little trouble in keeping it ajar.

A woman inside the room cried: 'Mind his head!'

Roger kept his right foot against the door to make sure they could not slam it, then drew back and threw his full weight against it. The door sagged inwards, and was stopped by a chair lodged under the handle. The woman cried out in despair:

'I can't keep them out!'

Someone came running up the stairs; it was Pendleton's driver, big and burly and middle-aged. He took in the situation at a glance, called: 'Wait for me,' and lumbered up, getting into a position from which he could hurl his additional weight.

The woman in the room screamed: 'David, be careful!'

Roger and the driver thrust hard against the door at the same time; there was a crack of splintering wood. The door opened wider, a broken chair fell to one side, and a woman was staggering backwards, visible only in the half-light of the evening. She neared the window where a man was climbing out in a peculiar way. As Roger steadied himself in the middle of the room, a bedroom, a man called from the grounds:

'Stay there!'

Another man, Jameson, called out as if in fear:

'Don't let him fall!'

Roger saw the woman thrust herself between him and the window, still trying to keep him away from 'David'; then saw that the man at the window was holding another man's wrists, and this second man was dangling out of the window. Roger took the woman by the shoulders, gripped, and thrust her to one side. She swayed out of his sight, and he forgot her. The man called David was obviously trying to lower the other to the ground. Roger rushed forward and leaned out, gripping the wrists of the dangling man. David struck at him ineffectually. All at once the man's full weight fell on to Roger's right arm, as David let go. Instinctively, Roger tightened his grip.

It had all happened so quickly there was hardly time to realize the danger. The weight of the man dragged Roger forward, and as the window-ledge came only halfway up his thighs, his feet almost left the floor. His heart gave one great convulsive beat. *Let go or fall out* rang like an ultimatum in his mind, but he was not really conscious of it. He saw the bushes, and a concrete path immediately below. He saw men weaving and dodging about, torches shining up into his face with little bright blinding orbs. He heard a car engine roar and saw headlights blaze, but neither mattered. The weight got too much, and the man he was trying to save slipped. Desperately, Roger grabbed at him, and in an awful moment, felt himself topple out. Then suddenly a powerful arm encircled his waist, and held him firm.

Afterwards, Roger realized that the danger had lasted only for a few seconds, but at the time it seemed like minutes. He thought vaguely of the things he had heard: the woman's 'Mind his head,' and Jameson's 'Don't let him fall.' Then he saw a crumpled figure on the concrete, and Jameson bending over it, dark head quite unmistakable. Others gathered round the huddled figure, while two men stood staring up.

In the room with Roger was a tall, lanky man, the woman, and two detectives.

Down below, a man said to Jameson: 'Is he all right?'

Jameson didn't answer, and Roger turned back into the room. The man, 'David', stood in a corner, shoulders drooping, eyes despairing. The woman sat on the side of a double bed, her face buried in her hands, and a detective stood over her. Yet Roger had a feeling that he was absolutely on his own, that no one else was even near. His head was swimming. That annoyed him, for nothing had happened, he hadn't been hurt. His heart was still thumping like a trip hammer and sweat had broken out all over his body; it was like being in a steam-bath.

He moved slowly, towards the bed, glad to sit on the edge, opposite the woman. He thought she was crying; certainly her shoulders were heaving. He fumbled for his handkerchief and wiped the sweat off his forehead, and then realized that his mouth was parched and had a curious, almost bitter taste. He saw a wash-hand basin in one corner, made the effort, and went towards it. His legs were like lead. He let the cold tap run, rinsed his face, filled a tooth-glass with the water, and sipped; it was tepid. He drank a little more, then put the glass back. His hand was quite steady.

He could see everything clearly now, and felt much better. He began to think, too. The man in a heap on the concrete ground outside the window might be seriously hurt, might be Lewis *alias* Van der Lunn. He wanted to find out. He wanted to question the man and the woman here. He wanted to know what had been going on.

'David' had a nasty scratch on his chin and a speckle of blood at his lips and nose, thin grey hair like a golliwog's, eyes screwed up. He was looking towards the woman, and as if oblivious even of the men who were watching him, he took a step towards her.

'Don't cry, Beth. Don't cry.' When she didn't answer, but stayed there with her shoulders heaving and her face buried in her hands, he swung round on the man on his right and shouted: 'Don't hurt her. Understand – let her alone. It wasn't her fault, she wanted to stop me. You can't do anything to her!'

Roger moved forward.

'I should think we could get her at least five years in prison,' he said roughly. It was difficult to get the words out because he was still not quite himself, but they came clearly enough and with a significance that the man could not fail to see.

'What?'

'You heard me,' Roger said.

'But it wasn't her fault – I swear it wasn't! She didn't know anything about it until yesterday. She tried to make me stop. Can't you understand?'

'I know that unless you can prove what you say she'll look as guilty as you,' Roger said. One part of his mind was waiting for news of the man who had fallen out of the window, the other concentrated on this tall, almost hysterical individual. 'Do you really want to help her?'

'You bloody fool, of course I do!'

'There's just one way. Tell us the whole story now: what you've been doing, what started it, why you kept that man here, why you tried to escape from the house?' Roger, suddenly himself again, nodded to the man holding the prisoner's left arm. 'Let him go. Do you write shorthand?'

'Yes, sir.'

'Take down what this man says,' ordered Roger. 'My questions and his answers.'

So it began, Roger's words quietly authoritative above the sound of the shrill tones of the prisoner, the woman's sobbing. From outside came the babel of men's voices, footsteps, the noise of cars coming and going; then suddenly the urgent ringing of a bell, telling Roger that an ambulance had just arrived. It could only be for the man he had allowed to slip from his grasp.

If that man died, whose fault would it be?

7

SICK UNTO DEATH

As the man, David, talked he kept glancing across at the woman, Beth, and occasionally twisted his long, scraggy neck round, as if as preoccupied as Roger about what was going on outside. The noises had tailed off but soon another car engine started; almost certainly the ambulance. Roger's questions were brisk and to the point, aimed at getting the story out of the man, David, quickly, and he was sure of one thing: emotionally upset with the knowledge of failure and worry for his wife, this David was more likely to talk freely now than at any time.

His name was David Arthur Bradshaw.

Beth was Elizabeth, his wife.

The man who had tried to head Roger and Pendleton off downstairs was his brother, Joshua Bradshaw; and the other, plump young woman was Joshua's wife, Rebecca.

The basic facts were that Joshua and Rebecca owned the hotel, and Beth lived here most of the time, helping her relations. David was a steward employed by the British Overseas Airways Corporation.

He swore that he did not know any details about the man whom he had lowered through the window.

'If you hadn't come I'd have stopped him from falling ...'

Roger let that pass, and asked:

'Who is the man?'

'All I know is his name's Lewis,' David Bradshaw went on tensely. 'Listen, I – I was forced into it. Blackmailed. I—' He moistened his lips, and then words poured out of him. 'You'll find out sooner or later; you may as well know now. I've smuggled a few bags of diamonds in, the people I've worked for threatened to report me if I didn't do what they ordered. I *had* to.'

He had been given tablets to mix in a drink for Lewis soon after the aircraft had left Johannesburg, he said. He tried to pretend that he believed they had been to help the man, but at heart he obviously believed these tablets, and others he had given the man during the flight, had caused his sickness.

'He just sat in his seat all the time, looking as if he was in a coma. He didn't get out at Cairo or Nairobi, just sat there, I tell you ...'

Someone, he swore he didn't know the man, had come to meet Lewis at London Airport. Bradshaw said he had seen nothing more of Lewis until, on the same evening, another strange man had brought Lewis to the hotel. This man had told Bradshaw to keep him there until given further instructions.

Next came a garbled story of family dissension: Joshua and Rebecca had wanted to send for the police, David had confessed to them, Beth had pleaded to give him another chance. Fear in case Lewis should die had made Rebecca send for a doctor without David knowing.

It was a pathetic story in its way, with a ring of conviction about it.

Only on one thing was David Bradshaw absolutely adamant: he said he did not know the names of the people he worked for, that the individuals who gave him the diamonds to smuggle were different each time, that he had never before seen the man who had brought Lewis to the hotel, and there was nothing at all he could do to help the police to trace him.

In David Bradshaw, even now that he had recovered from the worst shock, there was deep and burning fear. He would not admit to it, but it seemed to show in his eyes and make his lips twitch and his voice unsteady. It passed itself on to his wife, who had recovered from her paroxysm of crying and sat on the bed, dry-eyed, staring, a handsome woman if one could forget the pale traces of her tears and the redness of her eyes.

Roger put question after question, until he felt sure he had learned all they could or would tell him now. As soon as he stopped the questions, there was a movement at the door, and Pendleton came in.

'I've been questioning the couple downstairs,' the Divisional man announced. 'Like to come down and compare the stories, Superintendent?'

'I've told you the truth,' muttered David Bradshaw. 'Listen to me, can't you? It's not my wife's fault, she didn't know what I was doing. She wanted me to come to the police. For God's sake, don't blame her.'

'We'll need to see both of you at New Scotland Yard,' Roger said formally. 'We'll send you there, and if we can let your wife go after you've both signed your statements, we will. It won't be up to me.' It could be, of course, but there was no reason to say so. 'Take them down to a car,' he instructed the man who had made a record of questions and answers. He stood aside for them to pass, Beth with her head raised now in a kind of defiance, David with his head hanging, his big hands clenching and unclenching. As they were taken down the stairs, Roger asked Pendleton:

'How much of that did you hear?'

'Most of it.'

'Do the others corroborate this chap?'

'Pretty well,' said Pendleton. 'We know what the situation is here all right. As far as I can judge no one but David Bradshaw had any idea of what was going on until Lewis was dumped into the hotel. Lot to think about over that, haven't you?'

Roger said: 'Yes.' He made himself ask: 'How is Lewis?'

'Not so good,' Pendleton answered. 'He's on his way to New Westminster Hospital. You should get a report from there soon.' Pendleton looked round the rather dingy bedroom, with the blue uniform of a BOAC steward on a hanger behind the door, a BOAC cap, a battered suitcase with the BOAC label on it. The square of brown carpet was threadbare, two easy-chairs needed re-covering, there was a look of dilapidation and neglect everywhere. 'Better have a look round here, and then check the rest of the hotel. Like us to look after it, or would you rather do it with your own eagle-eye?'

'Let me have a report first thing in the morning,' Roger said. He managed to grin at Pendleton's obvious satisfaction. 'Good job you pinned that picture up early, Pen. God knows what might have happened if Lewis had stayed there another night.' He paused. 'Is it Van der Lunn?'

'Your dark-skinned pal thinks so,' Pendleton answered. 'He's gone over to the hospital. I got the impression that he didn't really believe what he'd seen with his own eyes – he didn't want to believe it was the man you're after.'

'I'll go and talk to him,' Roger said.

Downstairs, Joshua and Rebecca Bradshaw were still answering questions, the woman promising that they would do everything they could to help, swearing that they hadn't intended to break the law, that the hotel was absolutely respectable. Roger glanced at the Visitors' Register, and saw that it seemed to be kept in good order. He felt quite sure of one thing: if the hotel was run for illegal purposes, Pendleton and the divisional detectives would find out.

Roger went outside. The night seemed cooler and clearer now with starlight, and the glow from all the street lamps, the windows of the hotel and nearby houses, all seemed much brighter. Klemm was waiting for him. Roger shook hands with Pendleton and got in beside Klemm, who was at the wheel of the police-car.

'What happened to our driver?' asked Roger.

'Pendleton sent him off with Jameson.'

'Right. Let's go and see how things are at the hospital,' Roger said. He sat back for a few moments as Klemm swung the car into the side-road, then took a road across the common, towards Battersea and the Thames. Klemm obviously sensed that this was no time to ask questions, and drove with a casual skill which sometimes seemed almost to be negligent, but in fact never was.

They crossed the Thames at Battersea Bridge, beneath smoke belching out of the four great stacks of the power station, and with the lights of the bridges and the Embankment reflecting like newborn stars in the smooth surface of the river. They turned off the Embankment towards the new hospital, a mammoth place of glass and ferro-concrete, more like a hotel to look at than a hospital. The forecourt outside was small, but beyond it, down a slope, was the underground car park, the entrance a huge slit like an open mouth ready to devour all cars which ventured near. They pulled up outside, and Klemm asked:

'Want me to come in?'

'No,' said Roger. 'I don't think there's anything else for you tonight. Make out your report for the morning. It needn't be too detailed, just general. We'll go over everything then.'

'Thanks,' said Klemm. 'Er—'

'Yes?'

'Won't be working too late, sir, will you?'

Roger frowned. 'I'll survive. Take the car. I'll get one from the Yard when I'm ready.' He nodded to Klemm, and walked up the steps to the main hall of the hospital, where first the doorman, then the porter seemed like pale relics from the old world in this new one of glass and brittle silence. Only two nurses, smart in their uniforms, seemed to fit in here. But the men were helpful, and obviously regarded him with the awe that the police seemed to inspire in so many people. They had been expecting an officer from the Yard, and Roger was led by another porter along the wide, pale-walled corridors, past the closed doors which hid life's secrets, to a silent lift, and eventually to a floor marked *'Private Wards'*. Red lights showed over some of the lintels. A little convoy of white-clad people, two male nurses, two female nurses, a man in a white smock, and an attendant came along, the attendant pushing a trolley on which a man lay at full-length, unconscious. It wasn't Lewis *alias* Van der Lunn. Light shone from a partly-open door marked 'Sister', and the boy tapped at it.

A youthful, starched-looking woman looked up from a desk placed behind the door.

'Yes?'

'Superintendent West from New Scotland Yard, Sister.'

The woman's aloof expression changed. She stood up and smiled herself into being human, dismissed the boy, and said to Roger:

'I've heard so much about you, Superintendent.'

'Mustn't believe all you hear, good or bad,' said Roger almost mechanically. 'Is Lieutenant Jameson here?'

'We have an empty ward, so he's waiting in there. Would you like some coffee?'

'Yes, please. And if you could find a sandwich I'd appreciate it.'

'So you missed your evening meal, too,' the Sister said. 'I'll see what I can do.' Tall and precise of movement, she led the way along the passage which was empty and silent now. There were lights over some of the doors, and she opened one and stood aside.

Jameson sprang to his feet.

'Hallo,' Roger said. 'It looks as if we've found a home from home. Sit down.' He waved to the chair, then sat on the edge of the single bed in this small, square antiseptic room, with its pale-green walls and its metal bedstead and its spindly table. He looked across at Jameson, and saw that the man's face was drawn, that he really seemed worried and anxious. 'How is he?' Roger asked.

Jameson said very slowly: 'He is sick unto death, Mr West.'

'Is he really as bad as that?'

'Yes, sir. It appears that he has been under morphine for nearly five days, and that the doses have been very large. Also, when he fell from the window, he injured the back of his head rather seriously, and they are operating on him for that injury now. Have no doubt, he is sick unto death.'

If he died, whose fault would it be?

'And he is Van der Lunn?' Roger made himself ask.

'Yes,' answered Jameson bleakly. 'I cannot understand it. I cannot believe that he would associate himself with this smuggling, but—' He shrugged his shoulders with a gesture of resignation which made him seem very young. 'It will be some time before he can talk, even if he lives to talk at all.' He stood up and began to walk about the room. 'Did you get any information from the people at the hotel?'

Roger began to tell him, and was interrupted by a tap at the door. A dark-skinned nurse came in, shiny-cheeked and attractive in her blue frock and white sash and head-scarf, carrying a tray with sandwiches and a pot of coffee. She smiled brightly at Jameson, who had obviously seen her before. Two black, one white, Roger thought a little absurdly. The girl had a pleasant, soft-toned voice, and seemed a little shy. Or coy? As she went out, she cast a quick look over her shoulder at Jameson, not at Roger.

Roger said: 'A conquest.'

'She is very nice.'

'Yes.'

'She comes from Kingston, Jamaica,' Jameson volunteered, 'and she has been in England for two years. She likes it very much.' He seemed to brood for a few moments, and then went on: 'Will you tell me the rest, please? ... And please allow me to pour out.'

Roger picked up a sandwich.

'When do you expect to hear from the operating theatre?'

'They told me that there might be some news by eleven o'clock, and it is now half past ten,' Jameson answered.

There was no news at eleven o'clock, by which time Roger's story was told, the sandwiches and coffee were gone. There was a sense of anticlimax in the period of waiting. Sick unto death, Jameson had said. Why had this affected him so much? It was almost as if there was a strong personal anxiety, apart from anxiety to do his job as thoroughly as he could. It was ludicrous to blame himself for allowing the man to slip.

Footsteps sounded outside, and Jameson sprang to his feet as the door opened, but it was the coloured nurse, here to collect the empty tray. She seemed more positively coy than she had been before. As she went out, Jameson looked at Roger, almost smiling, as if something had happened to help him relax.

'Mr West, I must wait here, but there is no need for you to stay.'

'We should have the news soon,' Roger said. 'The quicker we know whether we've a murder charge on our hands, the better.'

Could he have saved that man?

8

MURDER CHARGE?

I T W A S after midnight.

Roger felt tired out, partly from reaction, partly because he had been up so early that morning. Now, the evening newspapers were spread out on the bed. The Jamaican nurse had brought in another, smaller armchair, for Jameson. There were two messages, one from Pendleton to say that there were no diamonds at the hotel, one from the Yard to say that Elizabeth Bradshaw could be released if he, West, decided that was the thing to do. Roger wanted to know whether this would be a murder charge before he made up his mind.

Footsteps sounded again; this time Jameson sat still, but his body tensed.

The door opened, and the Sister and a grey-haired man in a white smock came in; probably the surgeon. He was rather plump, rather too red-faced, a little like a bucolic young man whom some shock or insupportable burden had aged in a few short years. Now Jameson stood up, and Roger felt a quickening of his own anxiety. Why did surgeons and doctors often take so long in saying what they had to say? As the thought passed through his mind, he knew that it was unreasonable.

The Sister said: 'Mr McMurray, this is Superintendent West and Lieutenant Jameson. Mr McMurray has just come from the theatre after the operation.'

There were the usual formal pleasantries, during which Jameson was obviously drilling himself not to ask questions.

'Superintendent, as far as I can tell you, Mr Lewis has a good chance,' McMurray said. 'The operation itself has been successful, but his general condition could affect his recovery. I think it will be a matter of several days before we can say what will happen with any certainty.'

Thank God for that, Roger thought.

'But you are hopeful?' Jameson couldn't restrain himself.

'Yes, Mr Jameson.'

'I am very grateful,' Jameson said. 'Thank you very much, sir. When will it be possible for Mr Lewis to have visitors?'

'Certainly not for another two days, and it will be even longer before he can be questioned, no matter how important these questions may seem to you.' McMurray was quite definite, yet managed to make his pronouncement pleasantly. 'Will you want a man at the patient's bedside, Mr West?'

'Yes, sir.'

'You will arrange the necessary facilities, Sister, won't you?' McMurray nodded at the two detectives and went out, as if glad his duty was done. Jameson, obviously suffering from the anticlimax, kept moistening his lips. Roger saw how very pink his tongue was; it had a curious fascination.

The Sister said: 'There's a car waiting for you in the forecourt, I believe.'

'I'd like to use a telephone before we go,' Roger said.

He spoke to the night-duty superintendent at the Yard and arranged for a man to be at Lewis/Van der Lunn's bedside. There was something else on the tip of his tongue, but he couldn't bring it to mind, so he rang off.

Klemm had arranged for the car; Klemm was certainly anxious that he shouldn't overdo it. Did he give the impression that he was heavily overworked? He knew a lot of men at the Yard who had nearly cracked up, over the years. The approach of a nervous breakdown through overwork had been obvious to Roger and to others who worked with them, but had always come as a surprise to the sufferers themselves. Should he have a medical check-up? The idea that he might need one was surely an indication that he did. He tried to shrug the thought away as he sank back into the car, with Jameson by his side.

'Where can I drop you?' he asked.

'If you could stop at a bus stop—'

'Nonsense. Where do you live?'

'In Bloomsbury.'

'My place is nearer,' Roger said, and leaned forward to the driver. 'Drop me at Bell Street, and then take Lieutenant Jameson to his home.'

'Right, sir.'

'You're very good,' Jameson said. After a few minutes, he went on: 'I hope there will be an opportunity early tomorrow to discuss the inquiry together, Mr West. There are some aspects of it which I am sure would interest you and which I am sure you would find useful.'

Roger shifted back in his seat, studied the face which was so black, the eyes which shone brightly as street lamp after street lamp passed, and the full lips. Jameson was smiling, but it wasn't really a smile, it was an indication of some kind of nervousness.

'Why are you so worried?' Roger asked. 'Why is Van der Lunn so important to you?'

After a long pause, Jameson answered: 'He is a very good man, a very progressive man. It would be a bad thing if he were to die. And he is an important man in the economy of my country. We need engineers and men of vision.'

Roger said drily: 'That may be half the reason.'

'Mr West—'

'It's all right,' Roger said, 'if you mustn't tell me, you mustn't. Forget it.'

They sat in silence for a few minutes, constraint upon them for the first time. The car turned into King's Road, and gathered speed; Bell Street, one of the turnings to the left, was looming up. They slowed down and took the turn. The bedroom of his house was in darkness, Roger saw; Janet and their two sons would probably be asleep – he must be careful not to waken them.

'Mr West,' Jameson said as the car stopped, 'I hope I have not caused any offence. I am a very troubled person. I am troubled because there seems to be some reason to believe that Mr Van der Lunn might be involved in this smuggling of diamonds, and, if he is, then it will have grave repercussions in my country. Already there is more than enough to preoccupy the Government, such a scandal as this could be—' He hesitated, and then went on: 'Disastrous, yes, disastrous.'

'We haven't any proof that he's involved yet,' Roger said. On the spur of the moment, he went on: 'Like to come in for a drink?'

'You are very kind, but I must return,' said Jameson. 'What time may I present myself at your office in the morning?'

'Is half past nine early enough?'

'I will be there at nine-thirty,' promised Jameson. 'Goodnight, Mr West, and thank you.'

'*Thank you, thank you, thank you,'ank you, 'ank you, you, you, you, you.*' The soft voice seemed to fade into the distance, carried away by the purring of the engine of the police-car. Roger wondered why he stood for a few seconds and stared after it, waiting until the red light turned the corner, and then vanished. The noise of the engine and the echoing of the voice were gone. Roger turned towards the front door of his house, passed it, and went along to the back; he preferred to go in that way, there was less risk of waking Janet. He reached the corner and saw a glow of light at the farthest window on the upper floor; that was Martin's room. He smiled to himself, a little grimly. It was nearly one o'clock. Martin would have a full day at his college of art tomorrow, and yet he was up there, painting or sketching, oblivious of the time. Roger slipped his key into the keyhole, pushed the door open, and went in as the light flashed on.

In the doorway leading to the front of the house stood Martin, hand at the light switch, mouth open, eyes rounded. He was a powerful-looking youth, with a crew-cut which gave his face a rather unadorned look, and his eyes a surprised expression.

Suddenly, he grinned.

'Hi, Dad!'

'Hallo, Scoop. Come down to raid the milk?'

'Just a sip.'

'Don't forget not to drink out of the bottle,' Roger said, and they both laughed on a subdued note. 'How's your mother?'

'Well, I haven't seen much of her, really. She had a headache and went to bed early. She's all right, I think. She left some supper, and said if I was up when you came back I was to tell you you could heat it up, or have it cold, but you must have something if you haven't had dinner.'

Roger grinned.

'She guessed right again! What is it?' He moved to the gas-stove, and found a plate laden with steak-and-kidney pie and vegetables, on a saucepan half-filled with water. 'Cold, I think,' he said. 'Funny thing, your mother's is the only steak pie I can ever enjoy cold. Put the kettle on for a cup of coffee, will you? Then get off to bed, or you'll be a wreck in the morning.'

'*I'll* be a wreck!' Martin retorted.

Roger asked sharply: 'What do you mean by that?'

'Well—' Martin-called-Scoop was momentarily ill-at-ease, but soon he answered with a kind of earnest frankness which was all his own, and could be exasperating or commendable according to the parental mood. He took the electric kettle to the sink as he went on: 'You have been looking a bit under the weather lately, Dad. Mum says that if you don't ease off a bit you'll crack up.' He turned the tap and water spurted, but he twisted his head round to look at Roger. 'Do you have to work so hard?'

Roger grunted, and then said urgently: 'Mind that kettle!' It was already brimming full of water and more was pouring out of the spout. Scoop snatched it from the tap and water splashed on to the tiled floor, and over his own thick, white socks; he wore no shoes.

'Sorry, Dad!'

Roger said: 'Never be a copper. Your life is not your own. I took your mother out to lunch today, and found the Assistant Commissioner on my back as soon as I reached the office.' He put the plate of food on the kitchen table, and pulled up a kitchen-chair. As he began to eat, he reflected that Martin-called-Scoop-and-once-called-Scoopy was nearly twenty-one, that in many ways he was older than his age, more mature, more balanced in judgement than many men five or six years older.

The cold steak pie had that appetizing flavour which Janet managed to give to her cooking; he enjoyed it. Martin brought a cup of coffee to the table, and a mug of milk for himself. He sat down.

'What kind of a day has it been, Dad?'

'Tricky and highly confidential,' said Roger.

'So I shut my big mouth,' Martin said. 'Sorry I asked.'

From another boy, that might have sounded impudent if not insolent, but from him it was a completely honest reaction.

'Half of it's a diamond-smuggling job,' Roger said.

'Diamond smuggling,' Martin echoed, and sipped. 'Sounds pretty romantic.'

'If you'd seen what I've seen tonight you would think it was pretty sordid.'

'Smuggling,' repeated Martin. 'There's always something not quite criminal to me about that – unless the diamonds were stolen first.'

'They were stolen,' Roger said. 'First they were consigned to different diamond merchants and industrial diamond users round the world. You know what fragments of diamonds are used for, don't you?'

'Cutting tools – for cutting metal, and drills, and—'

'Good enough,' Roger interrupted. 'Some left South Africa but didn't reach the consignee – they were stolen *en route*.' That much he could safely say. 'South African police are sure they all left the country intact. There's a tight internal control over diamonds there,' added Roger.

'I know.'

'Good. Diamonds are sold through one group only, the quantity put on the market in any one year is strictly restricted, to help keep up the price. Here and there, fresh diamond-fields are discovered, and here and there supplies of diamonds which were lawfully mined are sold to dealers who try to smuggle them out whenever there's a sellers' market. So there has to be a tight control.'

Martin grinned. 'It's certainly a good job I'm not a copper. I'd be inclined to wink at anyone beating the monopoly and if the chaps got away, say good luck to 'em.'

'There's a man in hospital tonight, who might recover or who might die.'

'Because of the diamond thefts?'

'Yes.'

After a pause, Martin said : 'Oh, well, I'm glad I'm not a policeman.' There was another pause. 'Were you there when he got hurt?'

In an unguarded moment, and largely because he was tired, Roger said :

'I was damned lucky not to break my own neck.'

He was startled as well as surprised by his son's reaction. It wasn't just surprise in itself, it went much deeper. It conveyed a sense of alarm and of anxiety which reminded

Roger of Jameson's manner. Quite suddenly, Martin became a small boy again, a scared small boy because he had suddenly seen something which frightened him and which he didn't understand.

'Oh, forget it, it wasn't as bad as that,' Roger said. 'It's all in the day's work.'

'Yes,' Martin said, soberly. 'That's what Mum realizes. She's afraid, Dad. She told me not to tell you what she said, but – well, I think I ought to. I didn't actually promise.' Twenty-one, fifteen, eleven, he was all three ages in one single moment. 'She said that she worries enough about you at normal times, but she doesn't think you're right on top at the moment. She says she knows that you have to be absolutely on top of yourself if you're to cope with sudden emergencies. I tell you, she's afraid, Dad. She's frightened you might have to investigate some crime against violent criminals, and – and well, that your luck won't last for ever.'

Roger sat back, aghast.

He was silent for so long that Martin began again, miserably:

'Oh, I'm a fool. I shouldn't have told you. I suppose you'll say that she's a bit worried because of her time of life, or something; it's always difficult at this change period, or whatever it is. But honestly, Dad, she's really nervous in case something happens to you.' He looked straight into Roger's eyes, and then added very slowly and deliberately, so that there could be no doubt that he meant exactly what he said: 'I am, too. As a matter of fact I was talking about it to Richard only last week. Of course, *he* said I was dreaming it up, that you're right on the ball as always, but – are you, Dad? Do you really feel you are?'

9

MOMENT OF TRUTH

ROGER STARED into his son's clear, rounded, apprehensive eyes. Scoop obviously wondered whether he had said too much, and his, Roger's, first reaction was of anger that the boy should talk to him so. He almost held his breath. He must not show anger, must not show his feelings; he must be quite rational and unemotional about this. And Scoop wasn't a boy, remember. He was an intelligent young man.

'Dad,' Scoop said, 'I'm sorry. I know I shouldn't have said that.'

'Didn't you mean what you said?' asked Roger, stiffly.

'Well, yes, but – well, I know I may not know what I'm talking about.'

A warmth of affection, in fact, of love, crept over Roger and drove all thought and memory of anger away. He smiled, obviously much more relaxed, pushed his chair back, and said:

'Haven't we always had an understanding that each can say whatever he thinks, provided he finds a way of saying it nicely?' When his son gave a barely perceptible nod, Roger went on: 'So you said what you thought, and I'm glad that you did. Want an honest answer?'

'Well – well, if you feel like talking about it, yes.'

'The answer is that I don't really know,' Roger told him. 'I don't feel right on top of myself all the time. Occasionally I seem to get more tired than I used to, but it's only now and again, and it soon passes. I have to put a bit more effort into everything I have to do, whereas I used to do it without thinking. Maybe the new way is better. I'll soon be fifty, you know.' When Scoop nodded, Roger spoke more briskly, almost as if he was changing the subject: 'Do you think your mother is seriously worried?'

'Well, yes, sometimes.'

'Such as?'

'Well, whenever a policeman gets injured, or run down by a car, or attacked by crooks, the newspapers always play it up. When Mum reads the story she's always more thoughtful than she used to be: preoccupied, I suppose. She doesn't say much, but now and again she'll throw the paper aside, and mutter something like "I know he'll overdo it sooner or later." That kind of thing, if you know what I mean.' Suddenly, Scoop gave his broad grin, showing fine white teeth with one slightly grey, the nerve of which had been 'killed' while boxing. 'After all, Dad, you do stick your neck out, don't you? Fish and I have a whopping great file of press-cuttings about you upstairs, and were going through them the other day. We formed a mutual "Admire Handsome West" Fan Club, and decided you ought to have had the George Medal at least three times.'

'You must show me this file of cuttings one day,' Roger said drily. 'Now it's time for bed, and I'm tired out. Good Lord! It's nearly two o'clock.'

Upstairs, in the front bedroom with the lamplight breaking the darkness, and a glow spreading over Janet's hair and face, Roger moved very quietly, and Janet did not stir. He was not long getting into bed. She turned over, her back towards him. He lay on his side for a few minutes, physically snug and warm, the tensions and the tiredness oozing out of his body. He believed he would drop off in a few minutes. That was one of the things which he could rely on unless he had some really deep preoccupation, and tonight there should be none – thank God the man hadn't died. He had done everything he could. He had found Lewis/Van der Lunn, and that would please Hardy as well as South Africa House. Queer business, though – and Jameson was really worried. Pity if he started thinking about Jameson now. It was amazing how subconscious thoughts could keep one awake. No need to worry, though; he was almost asleep. dropping off, dropping off; he would get more sleep than those poor devils at the hotel, more than David Bradshaw, more than his Beth.

Beth Bradshaw!

On that instant, Roger was fully awake, all thought of sleep gone. He had promised to ring the Yard and say whether David's wife need be detained all night. He had decided to let her go if Van der Lunn survived, and had actually talked to the Yard and forgotten the message about Elizabeth Bradshaw. He could picture her sitting on the edge of the bed, her face in her hands, her shoulders shaking as she sobbed. Well, it was her husband's fault, not his; it wasn't his responsibility.

But it was.

He got out of bed, very cautiously, and Janet stirred; he half expected her to speak. He went out of the room, leaving the door ajar, and groped his way down the stairs, not putting on a light until he reached the hall. The telephone was near the kitchen and living-room doors. He was able to shut one door before he dialled the Yard. He was answered at once, but it was some time before Sharp, the superintendent-in-charge, came on the line.

'Hallo, Handsome, not in bed yet?'

'Just turning in,' said Roger. 'As Lewis is alive, I don't think we need hold Elizabeth Bradshaw. Tell her we'll want to question her again in the morning, will you, and let her go. You can send her back to the hotel.'

'Yes. Glad you called,' Sharp said. 'Bradshaw's pacing up and down in his cell like a madman, because he doesn't know what's happening to his wife. I'll fix it.'

'Thanks,' said Roger.

He smiled with relief as he replaced the receiver, went upstairs in the dark again, heard Janet's deep breathing and was relieved that she hadn't been disturbed. He slid into bed, turned over, and was asleep in a few minutes.

· · ·

It was half past eight when Roger woke. He lay on his own, vaguely realizing that Janet was not in bed, uneasily aware that it must be late, staring at the sky which he could see through a corner of the window, ears strained to catch sounds from downstairs. Suddenly he heard Richard's voice:

' 'Bye, Mum. I must be off.'

'Be careful with that car!'

'I'll be careful,' Richard said with a laugh in his voice. 'It's the other chaps you have to worry about. Say goodbye and hallo to Dad, or is it the other way round?' He went out the back way, and Roger got out of bed, yawned and stretched, heard the roar of Richard's small, very old MG, and crossed to the window. Richard was waving to Janet, who was at the front door, as the car moved on to the road. Richard was taller, leaner, and in some ways more alert-looking than Martin. Out of the corner of his eye he must have seen Roger at the window, for he waved and shouted:

'Hi, Dad!'

Roger waved back, Richard drove out of sight a little too fast and Roger went to the head of the stairs as Janet turned away from the front door. This morning of all mornings he had to be absolutely himself, to make Janet feel that he was completely self-confident and good-humoured. She was quite tall for a woman. Her thick, dark hair was flecked with grey, her eyes had a clarity that he had always loved; she was a nice-looking woman by any standards.

'Couldn't spare a cuppa, could you?' Roger asked. 'Shall I come down?'

'I've got a kettle on, I'll bring a pot of tea up,' Janet said. 'What time do you have to leave?'

'An hour ago.'

Janet laughed. 'Don't be a fool. Seriously.'

'Nine-fifteen,' Roger answered, although to reach the Yard by nine-thirty, when he had promised to see Jameson, he should leave by nine o'clock sharp. Some kind of concession was obviously needed, so he made it cheerfully.

'I suppose it could be worse,' Janet conceded.

She brought up tea, which he sipped between moments of shaving, washing, and dressing. He felt much brisker than he had for some time, although whenever he thought of the conversation with Martin he felt rueful. Janet showed no sign that she realized this; in fact, Janet had slept soundly and was looking and feeling at her best. If she had any particular anxieties she hid them well, and Roger found himself

67

wondering whether Martin had exaggerated; but somehow he did not think so. He went downstairs to bacon, eggs, sausages, tomatoes, and fried bread, and at sight of the piled-up dish, he laughed.

'Did someone tell you I'm starving myself?'

'Something tells me that you're going to be very busy today, and that probably means a sandwich and a cup of coffee for lunch. How did the case go, darling?'

'*Comme çi, comme ça,*' Roger replied. 'And if the radio or the evening newspapers try to pretend I was a hero last night, don't believe them.'

On the instant, alarm flared up in Janet's eyes, and he knew that Martin had been right, that fear for him was on top of Janet's mind. He wanted to eat up and be off, but if she showed any sign of wanting to talk, of needing reassurance, he would have to stay. For a few moments she stared at him, and he pretended that he didn't know what was in her mind. Then he gave her a hug and a quick kiss, and said:

'With a bit of luck I'll be home early tonight.'

Janet made no comment, and seemed to have recovered. He knew that she hadn't, of course. That she had simply repressed her feelings so as not to delay him. She made coffee, and he tucked into the breakfast, enjoying every mouthful.

It was half past nine before he left home. He decided to go along the Embankment to Westminster, and at the approach to Albert Bridge, found himself crawling in a long line, mostly of stinking diesel trucks, heading in the same direction. There ought to be a law against diesel fumes. The Embankment seemed to be getting noisier and busier every day. All the traffic lights were against him, and by the time he swung across Parliament Square and then turned on to the Embankment and into the Yard, he was as bad-tempered as at the end of a tough day. He saw no parking-place; everyone was parked in the courtyard this morning.

A man came up. It was ferrety-looking Detective-Sergeant Gorlay, still bent on pleasing him.

'Like me to park it for you, sir?'

'Er – yes. Yes, thanks.' Roger got out. 'Leave the keys at the front desk.' He trotted up the stone steps towards the front entrance, mollified by Gorlay's manner; blow hot, blow cold, that was the truth about his moods. He saw that it was five past ten, and for some reason was particularly sorry that he had kept Jameson waiting. Everyone else would know that it was unavoidable, but would the South African? He was nearly at his office door when another opened, and Klemm appeared, moving in a hurry.

Klemm pulled up with the suddenness and grace of a Spanish dancer.

'Oh, *here* you are.' Before Roger could respond, he went on: 'Hardy's been looking for you all over the place. Will you go straight up the minute you get in?'

Roger said sharply: 'One of these days you'll be caught saying "Hardy" instead of "the Assistant Commissioner", and that won't do you any good.' He saw Klemm react almost resentfully. 'Is Lieutenant Jameson here?'

'Yes. He's been waiting for at least half an hour.'

Roger nodded, and strode along to his own office, heard someone speaking, opened the door and saw Jameson sitting on the arm of an easy-chair, talking into the telephone and obviously concentrating on what he was saying. Roger drew back. He let the door close, and went straight to see Hardy. As he walked down the stairs he warned himself that he must not show any resentment, whatever Hardy said.

He tapped at the secretary's door, but there was no answer. He went in, found the room empty, went across to Hardy's office, tapped, and heard Hardy say: 'See who that is, Rose.' The door opened, and the secretary said:

'It's Mr West.'

'Oh, Handsome.' Hardy got up from his desk and moved towards him. His secretary slipped past Roger, and he could have sworn that she winked at him. 'I hear you made a hero of yourself again last night.' Hardy placed a hand on Roger's shoulder for a moment, a rare demonstrative gesture. 'If Van der Lunn had died, I think we'd have been in trouble. As it is, it looks as if we're in everybody's good books, which makes a nice change.' He motioned to a chair and Roger sat down with a feeling that this wasn't really happening to him. 'There are the two distinct problems,' went on Hardy.

'The disappearance of the packets of diamonds, and the kidnapping of Van der Lunn. We've obviously reason to suspect that they're connected, but can't be certain. The South African Ambassador is very anxious to find out. I gather from du Toit that you've impressed him as being openminded, and able to see this problem without any kind of – er – emotional prejudice.'

Hardy paused.

Roger said almost ruefully: 'Du Toit must have bought an awful lot of butter.' He just stopped himself from adding: 'What's all this leading up to?'

'Butter or blarney, they're impressed, particularly because we've found Van der Lunn very quickly.'

'That was a mixture of luck and routine.'

'A hell of a lot of our work is,' remarked Hardy, 'but we don't have to tell du Toit. The point is, I want you to drop everything else and concentrate on finding out whether the kidnapping of Van der Lunn was connected with the diamonds, or with his visit to London about oil surveying. Before another negotiator is sent out from South Africa the authorities want to know the motive. No one says so, but there's obviously some fear that it might be politically inspired, and so far there's no way of telling. What I really want you to do,' added Hardy with a broad smile, 'is find out that this *isn't* political! If you can do that, the air will be cleared, and we'll have a lot of people off our backs. So you have *carte blanche*. Leave no stone unturned and all that. Use as many men as you need – within reason,' the Assistant Commissioner added with a dash of characteristic caution. 'How long will it take you to put someone else on to the other jobs you've got in hand?'

'Not long,' Roger answered. 'They can always have a word with me if they're pushed. Any special instructions?'

'This is a job you've got to play by ear,' said Hardy. 'Make sure your ear's tuned in properly.'

10

PLAYING BY EAR

ROGER STRODE along the passages of the Yard as if new life had been breathed into him. That made itself evident by the length of his stride, the feeling that he could push aside everything that got in his way, the fact that a dozen aspects flashed into his mind, and he knew exactly what he wanted to do about every one of them. He pushed open the door of the office where Klemm worked with five other chief inspectors, to find Klemm there on his own, writing. He looked up.

'Tell Gorlay to come along to my office at noon, will you? And come yourself.' Roger let the door swing to behind him. 'Any bright ideas about men we could use on this job?' Before Klemm could say 'What part of the job?' Roger went on: 'We want a small team ready to work night and day on it until we find out the real reason for the attack on Van der Lunn. You, Jameson, Gorlay, a couple of DO's and another CI, one who won't get in your hair or mine.'

Klemm was grinning almost fiercely.

'McKay,' he said promptly. 'He's our best diamond-man after Mr Butterworth. Knows Amsterdam inside out, knows more diamond thieves and diamond smugglers than the rest of us put together – rest of us CI's,' Klemm added as a hurried afterthought.

'Do you know if he's free?'

'He's tidying up the evidence on that Hatton Garden job. Then he was going to have a week's fishing.'

'The fish will bite a lot better next month,' said Roger. 'Brief him, will you? I'm going along to my office, then over to Cannon Row. Is Jameson with you?'

'Patient as Job.'

Roger nodded, and went out: Klemm was already speaking on the telephone and the last words Roger heard as the door closed were: '. . . see if McKay's there.' Roger's office was only a few doors along. He thrust the door open so suddenly that Jameson jumped up from a chair at the corner of the desk, and papers he was writing slithered over the shiny surface.

''Morning,' Roger said. 'Sorry I'm late. What've you got?'

'I am trying to make sure that nothing has been forgotten,' said Jameson. 'Mr Klemm was good enough to allow me to see a copy of his notes.'

'What did he miss?' asked Roger, and laughed. 'Never mind – it would be a miracle if we didn't all miss something when things happen as fast as they did last night. Had any bright ideas yourself?'

Jameson was looking puzzled at Roger's manner.

'No, sir, but I have certain information for you.' When Roger didn't ask what, he went on: 'I have seen Mr du Toit, who is most grateful for everything you have done already. I took the liberty last night, after you had retired, of telephoning Mr du Toit and also my Colonel in Pretoria.' Jameson spoke as if he had made a local call, not one halfway across the world. 'It is now known that Mr Van der Lunn's apartment in Johannesburg has been burgled, and thoroughly searched, and many documents of importance have been stolen. There is one thing which we overlooked last night.'

Roger went very still. 'Is there?'

'Yes, sir, there is.' Jameson looked as if he hated having to say this. 'We did not search for any luggage which Mr Van der Lunn had with him.'

Relieved, Roger said drily: 'No. But we should have a report from the Division during the morning; they did all the searching at the hotel.' He ran through the pile of correspondence on his desk, and unearthed a sealed envelope with a *By Hand From SW Division* on it. 'Here's Pen's report.' He slit open the envelope and began to read aloud: 'Nothing of Lewis's found at the Common View Hotel except oddments taken from his clothes – handkerchief, keys, coins, stamps. Nothing of any importance ... Rebecca and Joshua Bradshaw state that when Lewis was brought to the

72

hotel on Monday evening he had only the clothes he stood up in, no wallet, no money, no luggage—' Roger glanced up at Jameson, who was smiling with satisfaction. 'They say that they didn't see the man who brought Lewis. Only David Bradshaw saw him, although there is a possibility that David's wife Elizabeth caught a glimpse of the man. A newspaper boy who was mending a puncture in his bicycle tyre saw a taxi arrive. A man answering Lewis's description was inside. The boy says David Bradshaw, in uniform, helped the passenger out and carried him upstairs. The taxi then drove off. Could have been a genuine taxi,' Roger observed, and went on: 'Ah! Pendleton is asking all of his people to report if they saw a taxi near Common View Hotel that night. He should have some news in this morning. Doesn't miss much, does he?'

'No one in your Force appears to miss very much,' said Jameson with obvious feeling.

'Now what else?' Roger asked, almost as if he were speaking to himself. 'Elizabeth Bradshaw returned to the hotel at two forty-five, that's about right ... Pendleton has questioned all three of them again this morning and their stories are identical with the statements they made last night ... Dr Abbott, who was acting *locum* for the Divisional police-surgeon this week was called to the house by Rebecca Bradshaw, that's corroborated ... He examined Van der Lunn and came to the conclusion that he was suffering from an overdose of drugs and wanted him removed to hospital at once, but David and Joshua Bradshaw wouldn't allow it. That was what made Abbott suspicious. So Abbott went back to the Divisional HQ to tell Pendleton he thought something was wrong at the hotel, and noticed the photograph pinned up on the board.' Roger looked up. 'Not much more we need from that. If you've any questions you want to ask, make a list and we'll talk to Pendleton this afternoon.'

'I will do that,' Jameson promised.

'What next?'

'I hope you will allow me to be present when you question David Bradshaw.'

'Yes, and we'll go straight over. He'll have to be charged formally in court some time today, but we have an afternoon hearing if we want it. Let's go over to Cannon Row. Have you ever been there?' he asked as he stood up.

'No. But I have often heard of it.'

'It's the nearest police-station to the Yard and does a lot of our chores for us,' Roger said. 'A night in the cell might have made Bradshaw remember a lot of things he forgot last night.'

The Station Superintendent, elderly and paunchy and somewhat cynical, said that after his wife had been released, the prisoner had settled down and fallen asleep. He had been woken with breakfast, but had dozed off again soon afterwards.

The superintendent sent for the sergeant-in-charge of cells, a middle-aged barrel of a man with an unexpectedly high-pitched voice, who led the way, jangling keys with absent-minded relish. An elderly man without collar or tie sat dejectedly behind the bars of one cell. Two were empty. In the fourth was David Bradshaw, who was sitting on the bed reading a magazine. He looked relaxed and rested – satisfied, Roger thought oddly.

Bradshaw looked up. He nodded recognition, glanced at Jameson with casual interest, and said:

'Thank you for being so considerate to my wife, Superintendent.' His voice was hoarse in a croaking kind of way.

'We're only interested in making the guilty pay,' Roger said prosily.

The sergeant unlocked the cell door, let Roger and Jameson in, and shut the door on them.

'Like me to stay close by, sir?'

'I'll be at least a quarter of an hour. You'll be within earshot, won't you?'

'Oh, yes.' The sergeant locked them in, and went off, his orders carried out to the letter.

Roger turned to Bradshaw.

'If you're being pushed around by some big shots, we'll do all we can for you if you help us find them.' He let this sink in. 'This statement—' He tapped a copy of the statement which Bradshaw had made and signed the previous night. 'It can't be true.'

'Every word is,' asseverated the BOAC steward.

'You say you have no idea who gave you the bags of diamonds or who collected them. But you've been at this game for months, on your own admission.'

'I tell you I wouldn't know the men from Adam,' insisted Bradshaw. He looked rather like a scraggy turkey with his long neck and big nose, as he darted round on Jameson. 'He might be one of them for all I know. A mechanic or one of the porters at the airport might slip them to me. Sometimes they'd be put on the aircraft in my bag – I always had to leave it unlocked. When I got the stuff to London and past the Customs, someone I'd never seen before would come up and ask for it. Or else when I arrived here, someone would be waiting for me, and I'd be told to leave the stuff in that old umbrella on the porch.'

'How did you know you were giving it to the right man, or the right man was getting it?'

'There was a kind of code word,' answered Bradshaw. 'That's what it amounted to, anyhow. Whoever spoke to me asked for "that piece of wash-leather" or told me where to put "that piece of wash-leather". It was a kind of joke, and after a while it seemed so easy I almost forgot there was anything wrong about it.'

'Last night you said that once you'd started you were blackmailed into going on with it,' Roger said sharply.

'So I was – at first. Then it became a kind of habit.'

'What threats were used?'

'They always said that if I didn't do what I was told they'd slip some diamonds in my baggage and report it to Customs,' said Bradshaw. 'I didn't know who they were, so I couldn't give them away. *They* were all right. And I knew that if my wife knew, she would have a terrible shock. Superintendent, what do you think will happen to me? How long do you think I'll spend in prison?'

'You could halve the time of your sentence if you helped us find your accomplices and employers,' said Roger.

'You don't take no for an answer easily, do you?' asked

Bradshaw with a flash of spirit. 'What I don't know I can't tell you.'

'Would you recognize any of these men again?'

Bradshaw hesitated. 'I might, I suppose.'

'Can't you be sure?'

'Not until I see one of them,' answered Bradshaw. He added with a note of desperation: 'Listen, it was like this. I'd be walking from the airport buildings towards the aircraft and someone would sidle up to me and push the packet into my hand or my pocket. Or I'd go and open my case and find something tucked down the side. Or I'd meet a man at a bar who wouldn't look at me but would whisper something about "wash-leather", so that I knew what to do. And I'd been warned not to take a close look at any of these chaps – I didn't want my throat cut.'

'Did you seriously think you'd have your throat cut if you let them down?' asked Roger.

'The way they threatened me didn't leave much doubt.'

After a pause, Roger said: 'Was it always a different man or woman?'

'As far as I know, yes.'

'Did you ever see the same man or woman twice?'

'If they were the same I didn't recognize them.'

'How often have you done this on average?'

'About once every couple of weeks.'

'For six months?'

'Seven months, as a matter of fact.'

'So you've been told what to do by over two dozen people – here and in South Africa.' Roger paused. 'Do you know what you're saying? Over twenty-four people are involved in this smuggling, not just one or two.'

Bradshaw said, almost savagely: 'That's right, and how do you know I'm the only steward they used? How do you know they don't use other stewards on the BOAC and TWA, and South African Airlines and KLM and Qantas, and all the rest who use Pretoria and Johannesburg and come to London? And if it comes to that, what makes you think the diamonds are smuggled only to London? Eh? What makes you think that?'

Roger said slowly: 'I didn't say I thought anything of the kind. Bradshaw, you're in deep trouble.'

'Don't I know it!'

'Deeper than you think.'

'What the hell do you mean?'

'I mean you know the size of this organization, and you know a lot more about it than you pretend to,' said Roger. 'You can still help yourself by telling us everything, but you're bound to make it worse for yourself if you keep on lying.'

'I'm not lying,' Bradshaw insisted harshly. 'Any fool could tell this was a big racket, and I'm not that kind of a fool. If they used as many operatives as that when dealing with me it had to be big, and if it was that big it was probably worldwide. Don't tell me you hadn't realized that.'

.   .   .

Bradshaw was quite right, this had all the indications of an extensive criminal organization with world-wide ramifications. So it could tie-in with the assignment Nightingale of *The Globe* was on, and with the diamond smuggling which Hammerton was investigating. There was little doubt that Jameson and the South African Embassy knew or at least suspected the truth. Jameson must have known. Hardy must have had a pretty good idea, too. He would not have been so pleased with the situation, du Toit and the Ambassador wouldn't have been so appreciative of the results of last night's activities, unless they had known cause for such elation.

Bradshaw was too preoccupied with his special brand of self-justification to notice Roger's tension. Jameson was standing on one side, somehow merging into the cell walls, part of the wall rather than one of the three people present. Roger's mind started to work more smoothly. What else should he ask Bradshaw? What was likely to break Bradshaw down – except danger to his wife?

Roger was already saying: '... what else did they tell you about Lewis?'

'Lewis, Lewis, what the hell's the use of keeping on about

77

Lewis,' croaked Bradshaw. 'I've been going to and from Johannesburg long enough to know all the big shots, so why don't you stop pretending about Van der Lunn. They just told me to give him these tablets to keep him quiet; they said they were sedatives and wouldn't do him any harm—'

'Who said?' interrupted Roger.

'I was called to the telephone at Johannesburg. A man told me I wouldn't have any wash-leather to worry about. I was to look after a passenger. He said I'd find some tablets pushed into my pocket as I left the telephone booth, and I was to follow the instructions on the label – one tablet every four hours for Van der Lunn. If you hadn't rushed me last night he would have been all right.'

'Why did you try to get him out of the hotel?' Roger demanded harshly.

'I had to try! I thought if I could get him away you wouldn't have anything on me. There was nothing at the hotel. You couldn't find what wasn't there, so all I had to do was get rid of Van der Lunn. I didn't realize you had the place surrounded, or I wouldn't have run for it. And I didn't throw him out, he fell. It was an accident, you can't blame me for that.'

'You'll be surprised what you can be blamed for,' Roger said gruffly. 'You'll be charged this afternoon with kidnapping Lewis—'

'Van der Lunn!'

'Didn't it ever occur to you that you might be wrong?' demanded Roger. He heard voices along the passage, and thought that someone was asking for him, but he did not look away from Bradshaw. 'Have you got a lawyer?'

Bradshaw was momentarily silenced. He moistened his lips, and then said in that croaking voice:

'Beth will see to that. Beth – Beth always looks after everything. She'll get me a lawyer.' In that moment he sounded pathetic.

Then, he saw someone behind Roger, beyond the steel bars in the passage. And on the moment of recognizing whoever was there, terror blazed up in his eyes. Roger swung round. The barrel-shaped sergeant-in-charge of cells was talking to a small man who was looking at Roger, and saying: 'Yes, it's a very urgent message.' He took his right hand from his pocket, but there was no message, only a gun. The movement was so casual that at first the significance did not dawn on Roger. The man fired twice at David Bradshaw, and then once at the sergeant-in-charge who leapt at him, striking at the gun. The sergeant cried out and fell back; the gunman turned and raced along the passage; Bradshaw simply crumpled up until he was a sprawling, straggly heap on the floor. Roger sprang to the bars and shook them and shouted:

'Stop that man! Stop him!'

He heard the clatter of footsteps, another shot, a thud as of a man falling. Then he heard Jameson saying in an anguished voice:

'He's dead, he's dead.'

* * *

One bullet had caught Bradshaw in the left temple, the other in the left eye. Death must have been instantaneous.

I I

BETH BRADSHAW

ROGER FOLLOWED the events of the next hideous hour on a teletype machine in *Information*, with Hardy on one side and the Inspector-in-charge on the other. The Information Room was as always crowded and busy, there were hundreds of other investigations and dozens of newly-reported crimes coming up on the teletype, the telephones and the map-tables. Everywhere the controlled, streamlined sense of disorder, which Roger knew so well, was very evident. Now all he could think about was the one case – his case, which had seemed completely under his control and was now spread to the winds.

The messages were brief and to the point:

Flash: Charge-room sergeant and outside-duty constable reported man running out of Cannon Row Police-station. Duty constable gave chase, and was shot in the right leg.

Flash: Sergeant-in-charge of Cannon Row wounded in chest, immediate report says wound not serious.

Flash: Man seen to rush out of Cannon Row towards Westminster Bridge and to leap on pillion of waiting motor-scooter, colour pale blue.

Flash: Scooter believed to have headed south on far side of Westminster Bridge. All Divisions alerted.

Flash: Police-surgeon stated that David Bradshaw was presumably killed by bullets fired at close range. Autopsy arranged for early pm.

Flash: No trace of scooter or rider or passenger.

Flash: Duty constable's leg wound not serious.

Flash: Condition of sergeant-in-charge of cells more serious than at first realized, now being prepared for operation at Charing Cross Hospital.

Flash: Pale-blue Lambretta motor-scooter believed to have been seen near Lambeth Bridge – being followed by Divisional car.

Flash: Lambretta motor-scooter overtaken, rider and passenger able to establish fact that they were not at Westminster at the time of the attack.

Flash: Man who attacked police and killed prisoner at Cannon Row now described as of about 5 feet 3 inches in height, sallow complexion, dark hair, dressed in Italian-style suit, tapered trousers, pointed shoes with low heels, narrow-brimmed embroidered trilby-style hat.

So it went on, until Hardy turned to Roger, and for the second time that day placed a hand on his shoulder, now in commiseration and understanding.

'We've lost the swine,' the *Information* CI said. 'Be damned lucky to get him now. I – what's this?'

Flash: Bullet which passed through David Bradshaw's temple now identified as a ·22 Italian-style correction Italian-manufactured bullet.

'Still got a chance, then,' remarked Hardy. 'Well, everyone's been alerted: all stations, ports, and airfields have been warned to look out for him. He may not find it so easy to get away.' But Hardy was not as optimistic as he tried to sound. 'I suppose it could have been worse. I hope Wardle's all right.'

'Wardle?' queried *Information*.

'The sergeant over at Cannon Row,' said Roger. He nodded to the inspector and went out with Hardy, acutely aware of the fact that everyone looked at him with exceptional intentness. It was inevitable that when policemen were attacked something happened at the Yard: a tense, keyed-up atmosphere affected everyone.

In the passage, Roger asked Hardy: 'Still *carte blanche* for me?'

'More necessary than ever, I'd say.'

'Oh, I don't know,' said Roger. 'I was half inclined to believe that Bradshaw didn't know more than he'd said.' When Hardy didn't answer, Roger went on: 'I'd like to go over to see his wife, and find out if she's got more information than she's told us.' In an undertone, he added: 'I wonder if she's heard.' There was a real possibility that the newspapers had the story, and had already been to Common View Hotel.

Twenty-five minutes later, he knew they had.

Half a dozen men were outside the door of the hotel, which had an even more dilapidated look in daylight. Two constables were on the doorsteps, keeping the men at bay. They swooped on Roger when he stepped out of his car, cameras pointing, lights flashing, question after question being flung at him.

'Did you see the gunman, West?'

'Were you hurt, Superintendent?'

'Did you try to stop the attack?'

'Who was the coloured man with you at the time?'

'Any news of Sergeant Wardle?'

Roger turned round from the steps, and said: 'The last news I had of Wardle was bad, and that makes me even more anxious to get on with the job.'

'Have you got the killer, Super?'

'Any hope of arrest?'

'If ever I give up hope of making an arrest I'll stop being a policeman,' Roger replied. He turned round and stepped beyond the porch. Another policeman was in the hall, and coming down the stairs was a remarkably dapper little man, a shiny, polished individual, wearing a black coat and striped trousers and glossy shoes, a Victorian solicitor's clerk of a character. He stopped on the bottom tread and was still half an inch shorter than Roger.

'Are you Superintendent West?' His voice was perhaps a little too cultivated to be natural.

'Yes.'

'I'm Abbott, Dr Abbott. Are you hoping to see Mrs Elizabeth Bradshaw?'

Roger's heart dropped. 'I must see her, yes.'

'I can tell you that you won't garner any information from her,' declared Abbott. 'She refuses to take a sedative; she does nothing but sit on the bed and cry. I have told her sister-in-law that I think the paroxysm will soon pass, and told her what to do once the poor woman is amenable. Very bad business indeed, isn't it?'

'Yes,' Roger said mechanically.

'I'm glad you weren't hurt, anyhow.' Abbott nodded and walked past Roger, then swung round as if he had been stung. 'Oh, Superintendent!'

'Yes?'

'Is this affair still to be kept from the Press?'

'No reason why you shouldn't tell them how the woman's affected,' answered Roger. 'If they ask you anything about the identity of the man, will you just say that all you know is that his name is Lewis?'

'Very well,' said Dr Abbott, and he turned and stepped on to the porch, a little ridiculous with his correctness and his polish. Roger found himself smiling; the law was helped on its way by a lot of remarkable and some very peculiar men. As he reached the foot of the stairs, Rebecca Bradshaw appeared from the door which led to the kitchen quarters and the owners' living-room. She looked pale as well as plump, but there was something different about her; she had washed her hair, and it was drawn straight back from the forehead and kept in place with a band over the top, so that it was severely straight from the forehead halfway across the head, and then billowed out in a frizzy mop. The style suited her. It showed her features up well, suggested that if she lost a few pounds – well, ten pounds or so – she might be a handsome woman with a fine figure. The tight-fitting black jumper which she wore accentuated the fullness of her bosom, the smallness of her waist and the sweeping curves of her hips.

'Good morning, Mrs Bradshaw. I'm Superintendent West.'

'I know,' she said. Her voice was strangely taut. 'We aren't likely to forget you. What do you want?'

'I need to talk to your sister-in-law,' Roger said quietly. 'I won't worry her more than I must.'

'You'll worry her until she kills herself.' The words seemed to have more bite because of the slow, deliberate way in which Rebecca uttered them; it was as if she meant to make sure that each one counted. 'You'll drive her to her death just as you took her husband to his.'

Roger said flatly: 'Shall I go up, or would you like to take me up?'

She pushed past him and led the way. He knew that he should be able to disregard her words, but they stung. It was quite right that he had taken David Bradshaw to his death, and that the police had done nothing at all to save his life. What use was it to argue that no one would have dreamed of such an attack? That there had been no warning? At heart, he knew, he should have realized that if Bradshaw could give information away he would be in danger. The truth was that he had been fooled into believing that Bradshaw had been on the fringe.

As he followed the woman, Roger noticed the fullness of her calves, the unusual thinness of her ankles, and her very small feet. She walked with a spring in every step, muscles flexing.

A man was speaking in the room on the right, the one where Roger had been the previous night. Rebecca tapped sharply on the door, pushed it open, and announced:

'Here's that man West.'

She stood aside, and Roger went in. Joshua Bradshaw, looking remarkably like his brother, was standing by the dressing-table looking down on Elizabeth. Elizabeth lay on the bed, her knees bent, curled up as if she were trying to go back to the womb in her search for comfort. She wasn't crying, but tears stained her cheeks. She was deathly, shockingly pale, and that was emphasized by her dark, wavy hair. Her eyes were open, and she stared straight ahead of her as if all she wanted to see was the dressing-table at waist-height.

Joshua said viciously:

'Why the hell can't you leave her alone?'

'If you want to hear what I have to ask her, keep quiet,' Roger said. 'If you interrupt I'll send for one of my men to take notes. That will make admissible evidence of everything she says – anything any of you says for that matter.' He glared at Joshua, who gulped and shifted his position. Anger still glowed in his eyes. He had a larger Adam's apple than David Bradshaw's, and an even longer and scraggier neck. His nose was larger and more hooked, too. In fact, he looked like a caricature of his dead brother, and it passed through Roger's mind that his wife must have found a lot of quality in him to outweigh his gobbler-like appearance.

Roger moved to the head of the bed, pulled a chair fairly close, and spoke very quietly.

'Mrs Bradshaw, none of us can help your husband now, but you might be able to help his memory.'

She did not shift her gaze or stir.

'I doubt if anyone else can do this,' said Roger. 'The fact that he was murdered so wickedly suggests that someone wanted to make sure that he couldn't talk to the police. Do you understand me?'

She didn't stir or look at him.

'So we're bound to think that your husband probably knew much more than he admitted. This is a vicious and evil criminal organization. If your husband wasn't really part of it, or didn't know how bad it was, there's no reason why his memory should be smeared.'

Elizabeth Bradshaw did not show any sign that she heard, did not even appear to know he was there. He hitched his chair closer, and resisted the temptation to look up into the faces of the other couple, who had been scared into silence by his outburst and were standing very still.

'If you know he was deeply involved but had been forced into doing what he did, then we need to know that too. It will lessen the slur on his memory and it will help to make sure that no one else is victimized like he was, that no one else suffers as you're suffering.'

Rebecca burst out: 'You're torturing her! Why don't you leave her alone?'

Now Roger had reason to look up at Rebecca, and so to turn away from that death-mask of a face. He remembered how Rebecca had suggested that her sister-in-law might kill herself, and was quite prepared to believe that she would try.

'If you think I'm torturing her, try to imagine what will happen if she doesn't help me,' he said. 'She'll be questioned day after day after day. She may have to give evidence when we've caught the murderer, and also when we've caught the murderer's other accomplices. Instead of getting this all off her chest now, she'll find it building up inside her like a cancer. I've come here alone so as to give her a chance to talk freely. What she says to me while I'm on my own can't be used in evidence. But if she doesn't talk freely she'll have to be formally questioned, and we'll have to take her to the Yard. Can't you make her see that this is the best way to help her?'

'*Help* her,' Rebecca said chokingly.

Then, for the first time, Elizabeth Bradshaw moved. She raised her head on the pillow, slowly, and straightened her legs with almost painful slowness. She kept moving her head until she met Roger's intent gaze. It was like looking into the face of death, except for her eyes, which were like burning glass, they were so fiercely bright.

'If it weren't for you, my David would be alive,' she said in a toneless voice. 'Now I've nothing worth living for. Nothing worth living for.'

After a pause, a long pause, while Rebecca stepped forward and Joshua made a strangled noise in his throat, tears began to well up in those burning eyes; they began to flow, began to pour. Suddenly the death-like face twisted into an awful expression of grief. Elizabeth's mouth opened, her jaws seemed to work violently.

Then she began to cry on a terrible, high-pitched note.

12

DEAD END?

ROGER WAITED in the hall downstairs, haunted by a mental image of the woman's face. He had left the room soon after the outburst. Since then, he knew, Rebecca had persuaded her sister-in-law to take some of the tablets which Abbott had left, and managed to make her drink some hot milk. Now, both the Bradshaws were upstairs with her. They had to be questioned, no matter what their mood. There was no possibility of postponing the interrogation, but that didn't mean there was going to be anything to relish about it.

The telephone bell rang.

The wall telephone was in a corner by the stairs, and Roger went towards it, lifted the receiver, and said in a formal voice:

'Common View Hotel.'

'Is Superintendent West there, please?' It was one of the operators at the Yard.

'Speaking. Who wants me?'

'Mr Klemm, sir.'

'Put him through.' Roger thought he heard a sound upstairs, but no one appeared. Almost at once, Klemm came on the line. He began to speak hurriedly.

'Sorry to worry you while you're there, sir, but two or three things need your attention. Mr Pendleton rang up to say that so far he hasn't had any luck with that taxi-driver. All the neighbours have been questioned, as well as some people who were on Clapham Common. It's a thousand to one chance of finding out who it was now – shall we drop it?'

'No. Keep at it. Ask the Taxi-Drivers' Association and the owners to help, too.'

'Right. Nothing on that motor-scooterist, either, I'm afraid – looks as if the chap got clean away. But if he's still in the country, we'll get him,' Klemm added hastily. 'The noon meeting here, sir – I've postponed it until two o'clock, as you're not back. Jameson's been sent for by South Africa House, but he'll be back before two. Is that all right?'

'Yes, good.'

'I've been in touch with Hammerton at London Airport, and he's preparing a complete file on all the suspected smugglers over the past six or seven months. People whom Customs have turned inside out. It's going to be a huge job, checking on all air-crews – in fact, Hammerton says it's going to be impossible except at intervals over a long period.'

'I know what he means,' Roger said. 'But we can't work only through him.' His mind was beginning to tick over smoothly, quickly. 'Make a list of all the airlines which serve South Africa from London, and lay on visits to all the head offices – I'll brief you with what to say to them later. Then we need to draft a memo which we can send to police forces in all the world's largest metropolitan areas, outlining the situation. In other words, what we've got to do is to make a skeleton plan and put it into operation as soon as possible. The thing we're after for a start is any unexplained increase in supplies or stocks of industrial diamonds, or changes in the ruling prices for them, anything to suggest that any market's been flooded lately. Is McKay with you?'

'Yes. Raring to go.'

'Get busy on this job between you, and make sure you have a couple of typists from the pool ready to type anything out at a moment's notice.' Now Roger felt that he was beginning to see the investigation in its right perspective, and it built excitement up in him. 'We want to get information from all major capitals about diamond thefts, especially packets of industrial diamonds, or missing consignments. Then we need information from all airlines which run South African services, telling us what consignments have been reported stolen or suspected stolen from their aircraft. Next, we want all insurance companies who've paid out claims checked – here and abroad. You get the drift? Draw up a plan of campaign with McKay.'

'Yes, sir!' Klemm sounded delighted. After all, it was the kind of job which any chief inspector would love to get his teeth into. Klemm and McKay doubtless saw this as a major stepping-stone towards promotion to superintendency, and if they helped to crack the case, they would deserve it.

'Anything else?' Roger asked.

'There is one thing.' Klemm said that in a tone which suggested that he wished there wasn't. 'The story's leaked. Once the news of the shooting in Cannon Row got out – a couple of Reuter's men were in the pub at the time, and they knew about it within a few minutes – we couldn't hold it back. The fact that Lewis is really Van der Lunn is known, too. The Back-Room Inspector is being besieged by Fleet Street men, and I gather that South Africa House also has its hands full. Nothing we can do to stem that tide.'

Roger said thoughtfully: 'It might help in the long run. What's our official statement?'

'Hardy – the AC I mean – wants to know what you think.'

'Three things in a hurry,' Roger said. '*First*, describe that scooter – the driver as well as you can, and the killer fully. *Two*, ask for anyone who knows David Bradshaw to come forward. *Three*, put out a description of Van der Lunn and ask anyone who saw him at the airfield or afterwards, and anyone who might have seen that taxi deliver him to the Common View Hotel, to come forward. All clear?'

'Got the lot.'

'Spread it around fast – it can be given to all the Press, television, and radio. Ask for full co-operation – oh, and build the thing up as a huge diamond-smuggling conspiracy.'

'Will do,' replied Klemm, and he sounded as if he couldn't wait to hang up and start carrying out these instructions. No one could doubt that he would put everything he had got into this; if there was a danger, it was that he would be over-eager, and perhaps miss something obvious because he tried to do too much too quickly.

'I'll see you,' Roger said, and rang off.

As he did so, he became conscious of being watched. Until the moment of ringing off, he hadn't been aware of it, but now he knew that someone standing above him had been listening. He did not look up. Whoever it was must have moved and made a slight sound which had been noticeable as soon as he stopped talking. Roger stepped very slowly towards the foot of the stairs. Soon Rebecca Bradshaw appeared on the half-landing, making no attempt to hide or to pretend she hadn't been listening. It passed through Roger's mind that Rebecca's husband often seemed to be the one to look after Elizabeth, and he wondered why. He moved back from the stairs and watched Rebecca coming down. He thought something had happened to change her attitude; certainly there was now nothing like the previous venom there had been in her expression or in the way she spoke.

'You don't lose much time, do you?' she remarked.

'There isn't much to lose. How is Mrs Bradshaw?'

'Asleep, thank God.' Rebecca smoothed that very flat hair down with her right hand; she had small, pale hands, quite as delicate looking as her feet. Rough hotel-work seemed the last thing she should do. 'I suppose we ought to be grateful because you made her break down; she might be better after this. It's about all we ever shall be grateful to you for.'

Roger said: 'Mrs Bradshaw, there are some aspects of my job which I dislike as much as you do, but it doesn't alter the fact that I have to do it. You heard me ask for all friends of David to come forward. I've got to piece together a complete picture of his life in the past year, say – I've got to know all the people he knew, everything there is to know about him. You and his brother can help more than anyone, if only you will. And the quicker we see this picture, the quicker the whole bad business will be over.'

She said: 'I daresay.'

'Will you and your husband be sensible, and give us all the help you can?'

'What about your well-known threat that if we don't we'll probably come under suspicion?'

'You're already under suspicion,' Roger retorted. 'The only way to help yourself is to tell the whole story. First I want to ask you a lot of questions, then I want to ask the same questions of your husband. If you're both telling the truth, the statements will be identical on all important matters, won't they?'

After a long pause, Rebecca said ungraciously: 'All right, let's have the questions.'

She answered him briskly and briefly, and apparently without any evasions, but if she in fact was telling the truth, she knew very little about her brother-in-law. He had spent much of his off-duty time here at Common View, but for all she knew he might have spent a lot of time elsewhere in London or anywhere in England without his wife or relations knowing. Whenever he had left the hotel they had assumed it was for the airport, but they had no proof.

'As a matter of fact, Josh and I have always wondered if he had a little bit of fluff on the side,' Rebecca said. 'He's like a sailor, got every chance of leading a double life. Not that there was ever any evidence, and God knows that Beth worshipped the very ground he trod on, as they say. If it ever came out that he did have a floosie tucked away it would break her right up.'

Roger said slowly: 'Maybe she isn't so fragile as you think.' Rebecca put her head on one side in response to that, but made no comment. Roger took a picture of Nightingale of *The Globe* from his pocket and handed it to her, regarding it as no more than routine. 'Do you know this man?'

Her eyes rounded, and even before she uttered a word it was obvious that the answer would be yes.

'Do I! He's a man named Knight, a commercial traveller. He's often stayed here lately. He and David got quite chummy – their nights often coincided. What's he been up to?'

.　　.　　.

It was one of the days when Hardy didn't go out to lunch. He was putting on weight, so he cut down on his eating whenever it wasn't too much of an effort. He listened to Roger, nodded, and said:

'So here's something else to get your teeth into. Keep at it, Handsome, but don't expect miracles. This job's been going on for too long to be solved in a day.'

Roger said half unthinkingly: 'From here, anyhow.'

'What's that?'

'If we're right and there's a world-wide organization there's also a heart to it, and that's probably in South Africa,' Roger said. 'If it's going to be stopped quickly it may have to be from there.'

'Is that a hint?' Hardy was half smiling, half frowning.

'Hint? I meant it as a simple statement of opinion.'

'I thought you were hinting that you ought to go to South Africa and sort it out from there,' said Hardy, drily. 'By the way, I've a conference this afternoon at the Home Office and I expect it will go on very late. Tomorrow I've got the Police Conference. I'll be available in emergency, but handle everything without me if you can.'

'I'll try to,' Roger promised.

He went out, thinking: '*Was* I hinting?'

He went down to the canteen for a hamburger and some coffee, remembering what Janet had said: it was amazing how often she was right. None of the people immediately concerned with the investigation was present. A few super-intendents asked odd questions, there was a lot of evidence of the grim determination of the Yard to find the man who had attacked a policeman in order to kill David Bradshaw. Yet Roger fancied that he detected a note almost of resig-nation; everyone knew that this particular killer was going to be very difficult to find.

He was at his office at five to two. Two minutes later, it was crowded, with Klemm, Jameson, Gorlay, and McKay. McKay was as Scottish as he looked, with sandy hair which curled a lot, but was spread thin over his egg-shaped head, a gangling figure vaguely like that of the Bradshaws, a Scottish accent on which twenty years in the Metropolitan Police had made little impression; Roger was so used to it that he hardly realized that McKay had an accent.

Gorlay brought in two extra chairs, and they drew close to the table. Klemm had drawn a rough graph, showing the air-routes from the Jan Smuts airfield, the main international airport of South Africa which served both Johannesburg and Pretoria, and lists of the companies involved. There were BOAC, South African Airways, Air France, Alitalia, KLM, Lufthansa, and several others.

Jameson, who had been to South Africa House for briefing, came back with more detailed information about the opera-tion of the Jan Smuts airfield. A plan of campaign built up quickly. Klemm and McKay had snatched the opportunity like drowning men at a straw. Roger made a few suggestions but wanted to alter nothing.

'All right,' he said, at three o'clock. 'The next thing is a draft of a letter to be sent to all the airlines, another letter to be sent to all the police, preferably with a questionnaire – questionnaires get the information if the questions are lucid enough. Get all three drafted. Get envelopes ready for im-mediate posting – we want to post these tonight, even if it's midnight. We'd better put some photographs in – of Nightingale, Lewis *alias* Van der Lunn, and David Bradshaw. We'll need to enclose a description of the Cannon Row murderer, too.' Roger noticed Klemm about to interrupt and then think better of it. He grinned. 'All right, you make up a packet of enclosures. I'll go through them when I come back from *The Globe*.'

Jameson also looked as if he would like to say something, but couldn't pluck up courage.

'Anyone any bright ideas before I talk to *The Globe*?' Roger asked.

'There is one thing which might be worth doing,' said Jameson.

All of them turned towards him, as if knowing that whatever he suggested would be worth listening to. Diffidently, he went on:

'First, we have an outline map of the world showing the airlines which serve the world's capitals from South Africa.' He pointed to one of the documents which had already been prepared. 'Attached to each we have the schedules of all flights made from Johannesburg to these world capitals. We surely need to obtain details of the crews of all the aircraft, and this is one of the items of information we shall obtain from the airline head offices. However, there is one thing which I learned at South Africa House. They can now tell us on which flights and to which capitals Mr Van der Lunn has flown in the past six months. These are, I fear, very extensive. I think perhaps it would be wise to find out if this newspaper reporter, Nightingale, has been to any of them about the same time.'

13

MORE COINCIDENCE?

NOTHING HAD changed at *The Globe* offices; there were the same doormen, messenger boys, and lift attendant. When Roger entered the outer editorial office, Faith Soames smiled at him and stood up, looking delighted to see him. She had the ability to make him feel that her interest was exclusively in him, and he wondered whether she had that effect on all men. As she opened the door of her uncle's office and stood aside for Roger to pass through, he suspected that she deliberately stood where she did so that their bodies would have to touch – as she had once before. Her complexion was flawless; her smile had a touch of rare intimacy.

She closed the door on Roger, quietly.

Soames was sitting right back in his big chair, one hand bunched on the desk, the knuckles lumpy with swelling joints. He might almost have been sitting there all the time since Roger had last seen him. He made the same gesture to get up and shake hands, and dropped back into his chair with a grunt which he tried to pretend was a cough.

'I'll tell you one thing, before you start in with your questions,' he said. 'My secretary is a kind of natural sex symbol, and she recognizes a challenging symbol in you. Most men she keeps at a distance, can't even bear to let them touch her. Be careful, she's a minx with advanced views.'

Roger said drily: 'With a broad-minded uncle, I gather.'

'What's being broad minded?' asked Soames. 'She's an attractive young female, you're a handsome male. Do I have to be broad minded to acknowledge the fact that male and female are mate-worthy? But you didn't come here to talk about Faith. Have you found Nightingale?'

'No,' said Roger. 'But a man who was by way of being a friend of his was murdered today.'

Soames did not speak, but his big lips parted, and then closed very tightly together. They were silent for what seemed a long time, before he said:

'Unless my staff's slipping, there's only been one murder in England today. David Bradshaw?'

'Yes.'

'Nightingale doesn't make friends easily.'

'Unless he cultivated friendship deliberately,' Roger said. 'Mr Soames, one of two things seems to be certain. Either Nightingale was associated with David Bradshaw over the smuggling, and pretended to be a commercial traveller and went to Common View Hotel to meet Bradshaw as an associate, or else he suspected Bradshaw and made a point of going to the hotel whenever Bradshaw was there. It would be easy for him to find out what crews were on the aircraft coming in to London.'

Soames reflected, and then said: 'My money is on the probability that he suspected Bradshaw and scraped an acquaintance in order to obtain evidence about the case. He told me he was getting close. If he believed Bradshaw was a diamond thief or smuggler, then he was very close to the fringe, but not to the heart of the conspiracy.'

'My money's not on one or the other,' Roger replied. 'But I hope you're right. I'd hate a top Fleet Street man to be involved in this.'

'Don't believe it's even possible, especially with Nightingale,' Soames declared. 'Any other evidence involving him?'

'You might have some. I want to know where he's been overseas in the past six months. You told me that he could go wherever he liked, and had instructions to break this case no matter where it took him. Where did it take him?'

'You must have some reason for asking that.'

'When I know the answers I'll tell you what I can,' Roger said.

Soames grunted, leaned forward and flicked up the switch on the inter-office talking-box. Without waiting for Faith to say anything, and while staring straight into Roger's eyes, he said:

'The good Superintendent wants to know where Jim Nightingale has been in the last six months – especially when he's been out of the country. You should have that information handy, and what you haven't got, get quick. I've the Editorial group session for the next hour, so give Mr West all the help he needs and all the information he asks for. Also give him some tea and try to worm some information out of him – I think he's holding out on us.'

He paused and grinned. Then:

'Come in here as soon as you've got the files,' he ordered. Immediately he flicked the little handle down, and then began his cumbersome movements, out of his chair and on to his feet, followed by the painful walk to the communicating door, with the thick stick in his hand. He pushed the door open just as he had on the previous occasion, and this time spoke to someone who was in the board-room. The door swung to. Roger heard a murmur of voices, but could not distinguish the words. He waited for a long time, half amused by what Soames had said about his niece; it was almost as if he had deliberately intended to make Roger aware of the girl's quite exceptional attractiveness.

Suddenly she came in, carrying tea and six cakes, oozing with cream, on a silver tray. Cups rattled pleasantly as she put the tray down on a corner of the littered desk, and pulled up a chair.

'These are my uncle's favourites,' she said. 'Cream slices and chocolate *éclairs* – at least he doesn't have to worry about his diet. It must be miserable to have to watch your weight.'

'I wouldn't know,' said Roger.

'Milk and sugar?'

'Just milk.'

'And you don't watch your weight,' Faith scoffed. She was as natural as if she were his own daughter, and it passed through Roger's mind that if she were ten years younger, perhaps even five years younger, she would be exactly the kind of girl he would like Martin or Richard to fall in love with. She poured out. 'Do you like to relax over tea, or do you mix business with pleasure?'

'I do all my relaxing at home,' Roger said mildly.

'And faithful, too!' She handed him his cup and pushed the cakes towards him, then sat back in a small armchair, stretching out her long, slim legs; there was something feline about her manner and her movements. 'Well, let us proceed.' She picked up a sheet of paper and began to read: 'Our special correspondent James Nightingale was assigned to the mystery of the smuggled diamonds on March 27th, which means that he has been engaged exclusively on this case for six months. In that time he had made flights to the following countries: South Africa, twice, the United States (New York) twice, the Argentine (Buenos Aires) once—'

'Do you know the dates?'

'Do you need them now?'

'Please.'

She began to recite them, giving the impression that she expected him to challenge her, but he did not. His greatest difficulty was to keep a poker face, for the dates coincided, one after another, with those on which Van der Lunn had visited the same cities, although the South African had made many other visits. Van der Lunn had always been based in Johannesburg and Nightingale in London, but it was surprising how often they had been in the same places at the same time; he might have missed one or two, Roger knew, but he estimated nine such coincidences.

Faith was looking at him as if she was no longer quite so sure of herself.

'I assure you that my memory is quite reliable,' she said.

'I'm sure it is, but I'm not so proud of mine. Have you got all those written down?'

'Yes.' She handed him the sheet of paper; the details were typed without blemish. Instead of drawing back into her chair, she leaned on the edge of it, towards him. Today she wore a pale-green linen dress with a round neck, and as she leaned forward the neckline drooped forward. It was impossible for Roger not to see that she wore that kind of brassière which supported the lower but not the top part of her breasts, and in a swift, quite compulsive glance he saw how beautifully shaped they were, saw too the smooth white skin, the shadow between. He looked up and into her eyes; she was smiling quite naturally.

'After all,' she said, 'I was told to seduce you, wasn't I?'

'After all,' Roger retorted with an effort, 'your uncle wasn't to know that half the wicked women I have to deal with think they're experts in seduction.'

Her expression changed and she drew back instinctively; he expected her to jump up, or at least move her chair back, was prepared for something like the outburst he had suffered from Rebecca Bradshaw only a few hours earlier. Faith's eyes were narrowed, and her lips pressed tightly together, and it seemed a long time before she spoke; but once speaking she relaxed, and the smile returned to curve her lips and warm her eyes.

'Handsome, I think I would really love to get to know you. You're quite the man of steel. Can you tell me why you're so anxious to find out where Jim Nightingale has been?' When Roger didn't answer at once, she went on: 'I don't mind admitting failure to myself, but I should hate my uncle to think that I failed so utterly.'

Roger laughed. 'I don't think it would surprise him. He knows a lot about policemen. I can tell you, off the record. It has to be off the record.'

'I promise.'

'Van der Lunn has been to these cities, too, and sometimes his visits have coincided with Nightingale's. Interesting, isn't it? I read through Nightingale's reports, but tell me something else.'

'If I can.'

Roger picked up a cream slice with a small fork, placed it on a plate, and tried to cut it; cream and jam filling oozed out. He ate a little, watching the girl all the time, and when he was halfway through the slice, he asked:

'Why was Nightingale assigned to this particular case?'

'He was sacrificed on the altar of the Great God News.'

'What made this case such big news?'

'I wonder if my uncle would want me to tell you that,'

mused Faith, and after a pause she went on: 'I don't think he would mind.' She took a tiny handkerchief from a pocket just below the waist of her dress, leaned forward again, and gently wiped Roger's lips. 'If you prove to be a messy eater I may have to change my mind about getting to know you. There have been some indications that South Africa has been short of foreign exchange, and my uncle wondered whether this smuggling was being condoned by the Government, and whether foreign currency was being earned as a result of it. Anything which might be a slap in the face for the Nationalist Government always was food and drink to him, but he would have to be absolutely sure of his facts before printing anything.'

'And he hasn't printed anything?'

'I must put you on the free list for *The Globe*,' Faith said. 'No, he hasn't printed anything. Jim Nightingale was following up every angle, remember. As I've pointed out several times, he is a very good newspaperman. In fact, I think he's one of the very best, and Fleet Street seems to share that opinion.'

'Meaning?' asked Roger.

'Think,' urged Faith.

In spite of himself, Roger laughed. 'If such a brilliant newspaperman couldn't find anything to print in support of this theory, there wasn't likely to be much support or justification.'

'Clever boy,' mocked Faith.

'Yes, aren't I?' Quite suddenly, and taking her by surprise, Roger got to his feet. He gathered up all the papers and tucked them into his briefcase, talking as he did so. 'Well, I must be off, cream cakes or not. I've at least two conferences before I can go home tonight. Thank your uncle for me, won't you?'

'Aren't you going to thank me?'

'Of course,' said Roger. She was leaning back in her chair, looking as chaste and modest as a girl could. He bent down and kissed her lightly on the forehead. 'Thank you very much,' he said. 'For everything.' He wrinkled his nose at her, and then went to the door, opening it before she was out of her chair. He turned round to see what the effect was on her; he wasn't quite sure. She was biting her underlip, but her eyes seemed to be laughing at him.

'Goodbye,' he said, and went out.

As he went down in the lift, as he stepped into Fleet Street, chock-a-block with traffic in the evening rush hour, as he sat back in the police-car and was driven slowly and frustratingly back to the Yard, he kept seeing a mental picture of Faith Soames. One word kept recurring to him, not now and again but time after time: the word was: 'desirable'.

·　　·　　·

Klemm, McKay, Jameson, and Gorlay were waiting for him in his office, and the two CI's seemed almost smug. When he saw what they had done, he conceded that smugness was almost justified. The questions to the police, airport police, and airline companies were reduced to the absolute minimum. Each question was phrased so that the recipient could answer quickly and simply. No one was going to find this a red-tape job. The one to the police forces read:

1. *Have you been requested to investigate the loss of any parcels of diamonds of any kind in the past twelve months?*

   If so, please state:

2. *How many such requests have there been?*

3. *From which country was each parcel consigned?*

4. *Were they shipped by*

   (a) *Air*
   (b) *Sea*
   (c) *Rail*

5. *Who requested the investigation?*

6. *What was the estimated value of each packet?*

7. *Did you recover the diamonds?*

8 *Were the thieves caught? If so, please name them.*

9. *Can you name any suspects, confidentially?*

10. *If more than one case, have you reason to believe the same people were involved?*

11. *If known, please state insurance company affected.*

12. *Have you any reason to suspect that diamonds have been lost by firms which acquired them unlawfully?*

The questions to the other authorities were as succinct.

Roger wished Hardy was in his office, so that he could vet them, but he wasn't, and Roger did not hold anything back. He made a few minor changes, then gave the word to have them mailed. 'Add twenty-four hours to the normal time needed for delivery, and then start telephoning,' he ordered. 'The first dozen replies will give us an indication of how things are going.'

Once the rush was over, it was surprising how flat the situation seemed. He tied up all the loose ends, spoke to du Toit twice, and spent a session with the Embassy's Commercial Attaché. Hardy, still benign, approved what he had done. No reports of interest came in, but there seemed reason for hope – until the Hampshire police reported that both men and the motor-scooter had flown from Hurn Airport to Cherbourg the previous evening. They might now be anywhere in Europe – or they might be flying to any part of the world.

.   .   .

After this had been reported to the team, quite suddenly Roger was alone in his office with Jameson.

He sensed that the South African had stayed behind for a purpose. Roger had a strange thought: that a lot of people would look at Jameson and feel that he was the perfect specimen of his race, just as Faith Soames seemed the perfect specimen of physical womanhood.

'There is a matter I have to report to you personally,' Jameson said.

Roger sat up. 'What is it?'

'It is to do with Mr Nightingale.'

Every thought but of Nightingale faded from Roger's mind as he waited.

'Mr Nightingale has been arrested in Pretoria and is being questioned at Police Headquarters in connection with the diamond smuggling,' Jameson announced. 'Nothing has been said to the Press, and nothing will be said until you have advised Pretoria what you think should be released. It appears that Mr Nightingale presented a false passport at the Johannesburg Airport, hence his detention. His subsequent arrest was due to the fact that industrial diamonds were found in his baggage.'

14

ORDER FROM HARDY

ROGER COULD picture old Soames, sitting back, so sure of Nightingale's integrity. He could picture Faith, equally sure, almost laughing at him for suggesting that the reporter might be involved. This news from Pretoria was not conclusive but it would shock Soames, and would mean that Nightingale's activities would have to be closely checked. He sat back, looking up at Jameson, who gave the impression that he so often did; that he was anxious for approval of his action, and perhaps a little fearful of having done the wrong thing.

Roger rubbed the back of his head, and began to smile.

'I'll have to check with the AC, but I should say this news wants releasing at once – and it ought to be a scoop for *The Globe*.' He leaned forward and picked up the receiver and asked: 'See if you can get me Mr Hardy at his home, will you?' As he replaced the receiver, he waved to an upright chair with a padded seat. Jameson sat down. 'What would you advise?' Roger asked him.

'The same as you, Mr West. I am never happy when news is held back. The wrong motives are too often imputed.'

'And we have enough problems dealing with the right ones,' Roger remarked drily. He pulled the graphs and the questionnaires towards him, looked through them again, and went on: 'I don't think we've missed much, but it will be a couple of days before we get the information we've asked for. If I had my way I'd send a man to every capital, then we'd get what we want in a few days.'

'Is there any hope of doing that?' asked Jameson.

'Not the slightest.'

'Mr West, there is one thing I would like to suggest,' said Jameson. 'I have already mentioned it to Mr du Toit, without committing anyone to any particular course of action. I think you should go to Pretoria and see Nightingale, as well as study the situation from South Africa. Some aspects of it may show up in a new light. I can believe that it would be impossible to send a man to every city, but do you think there is any chance of you going to my country?'

Roger looked at him very intently.

'Is this your suggestion? Or du Toit's?'

'It is like many things – a suggestion from me with which he is in full agreement,' said Jameson. He gave his diffident smile. 'He particularly asked me to find out what you would think personally if such a suggestion was made. Would you object, sir?'

Roger grinned. 'I'd jump at the chance – and even if I didn't I'd have to go wherever I was told.' The idea already had an attractive look about it, and he remembered Hardy's 'Was that a hint?' which suggested that even early this morning, long before the news of Nightingale's arrest, the possibility had been in the Assistant Commissioner's mind.

The telephone bell rang.

'That'll be Hardy.' He snatched off the receiver, and the operator said:

'I'm sorry, Mr West, but Mr Hardy isn't at home. Nor is Mrs Hardy. They are at some function, and are not expected back until after midnight. I think it might be possible to find out where they are, if you would like me to.'

'No,' decided Roger. 'Have a message left asking Mr Hardy to ring me at my home whatever time he gets back, will you? ... Thanks ... And call my wife and say I'll be home in about half an hour. She – hold on a moment.' He covered the mouthpiece with his hand and looked across at Jameson. 'Would you like to come home with me and talk the case out over a meal?'

'I am most grateful, but I cannot,' said Jameson.

'Another time ... Just give my wife that message,' Roger said to the girl, and rang off. He stood up, walked to the window and looked out on to the river. He remembered crossing the bridge last night, and seeing the lights reflected in just the same way as now. He turned again as Jameson stood up. 'I'll call Soames of *The Globe* and tell him, but I won't release the story generally until I've had a word with Mr Hardy. Will that suit your people?'

'I am sure it will,' approved Jameson. 'What time will you be able to work on this case tomorrow, Mr West?'

'Let's say ten o'clock.'

'I will be here, or I will send a message. Goodnight.' Jameson went out, backing from the door and closing it quietly. Everything he did was quiet and deliberate.

Roger squatted on the side of the desk and asked the operator for *The Globe*. He wondered if Faith would answer him, and as the thought entered his mind his heart began to beat faster than usual, and the very fact made him angry. There were a lot of noises on the line – this was one of the busiest times for a newspaper which was just going to bed.

'Mr Soames's office.' Whoever it was, it wasn't the old man's niece.

'Ask him to speak to me at once,' Roger said. 'This is Superintendent West ... Hallo, Mr Soames ... Yes, she looked after me very well, thanks ... Yes, it's still off the record, but I have something else you can use if you want to. It won't be released for some time to the other newspapers, not in time to use in the morning's editions, anyhow. Ready?'

'Ready for some catch,' Soames said. 'You don't hand out scoops for nothing.'

So he had no idea of what was to come.

Roger wished he could be in the office to see the old man's

face as the story was told. Instead, he had to guess the way the thick lips tightened, just as they did when Soames moved and his joints hurt him. The silence lasted for a long time, so the shock effect was probably very great.

At last, the response came. In a harsh voice which sounded as if it was some distance from the mouthpiece, Soames said:

'They say they found diamonds in Nightingale's baggage?'

'Yes.'

'I wonder if they did, or whether they're lying.'

'If the Pretoria police tell me that they found diamonds in his baggage, then I believe them,' Roger said flatly. 'There's no point in evading the issue. If they say he was travelling with a false passport, I believe that too. Did he often use a false passport?'

Soames didn't answer.

Roger said gruffly: 'If he did and you knew about it, you were asking for trouble. I haven't been able to talk to Hardy yet – that's why I haven't released this. Pretoria's left it to us. All they ask for is simultaneous release. That's fair enough.'

'Yes.' Soames still sounded a long way from the mouthpiece; it would be easy to believe that he was too shocked to grasp all the implications of the situation. But in fact he wasn't, for he went on: 'I'll send someone out to Pretoria to talk to them and to interview Nightingale. You can tell your fine friends that if they don't let us talk to him we'll make a bigger song and dance than they've heard for a long time.'

'Soames,' Roger said, 'why don't you accept the fact that one of your employees acting on your behalf and with your knowledge has got himself into serious trouble? What you want from Pretoria are concessions, and if you write or say anything to put their backs up you can't blame them if they turn nasty. Will you use the story in the morning?'

'I'll print it,' Soames growled. 'I won't make much comment. Thanks for all you've done. I appreciate it.' When he rang off, it was easy to imagine him dropping back into his chair, grunting, staring under his bushy brows at the wall in front of him.

Nothing else came in.

Roger went downstairs, and found his car without anything parked within yards of it. Two or three men said goodnight and he nodded mechanically, for he was so preoccupied about the new situation and the possibility that he would be sent to South Africa. Between now and the time Hardy was told about this, he had to make up his own mind whether he thought it would be the right thing to do; it would be right only if it seemed likely to bring the inquiry to a quicker end.

Nightingale was a key witness; obviously it was essential to talk to the newspaperman, and equally Pretoria couldn't be expected to release a suspect against whom there was so much evidence.

Roger drove out on to the Embankment and past the Houses of Parliament, along the Embankment at Millbank. There was very little traffic, nothing remotely like the nightmare of the morning, and he was home in ten minutes. Richard's battered green MG stood outside the house, but the garage entrance was clear. Roger drove in, but didn't close the doors; Richard would do that – or Scoop, if he didn't walk dreamily past without noticing they were open. Roger went round the back way, and heard Richard's deep, very pleasant voice, saying something which he couldn't catch. Janet laughed. Richard made some retort and Janet's laughter became deeper. Roger opened the kitchen door, to hear Richard say:

'It's fantastic! There am I, sitting in state, with my name on the door, and except for the really big shots, everyone taps before they come in.' The lad was standing by the larder, and tapping the door lightly. Suddenly his tone of voice altered and he declaimed: 'Come in ... And I'm banging away on the typewriter so I just wave them to wait ... Then whoever it is says "Squire" – they all call me Squire these days; it's a studio joke. And the really funny thing was this morning. Someone tapped, so I did my stuff and rattled away a letter and then turned round – and Harry was standing watching me, looking like a statue. Harry – my boss! I couldn't tell whether he was amused or not, until I realized he must have been pulling my leg, or he wouldn't have tapped . . . Why, hallo Dad!'

'Roger!' exclaimed Janet. 'I didn't hear you.'

'Go on, Fish,' said Roger.

'I've finished, really,' said Richard hastily. He was tall, nice-looking in a lean-faced way, had a good colour, and dark curly hair. In that second Roger saw Faith as if she were standing beside the boy, and wondered how they would get on together. Richard-sometimes-called-Fish was now twenty, and he looked two or three years over his age sometimes. He had fallen on his feet in a studio near Watford, and was working with the script supervisor on a police series for television: 'Harry' was his chief, for whom he had formed a great admiration. 'Harry just started calling me "Squire", that was all. . . .'

Soon, Roger asked: 'How's work going?'

'Pretty well, I should think. I've started on a scene in a script, goodness knows whether it's what Harry wants, but I think it's better than the last one which he said was nbg. Only he didn't put it quite like that! I say, I promised to go and collect Scoop from that lecture. I'll be seeing you.'

Richard went out of the house like a rocket, and soon the engine of his car snorted. Janet was putting cold ham, pork-pie, pickles, bread, butter, and cheese on the kitchen-table, while Roger rinsed his hands and face at the kitchen-sink. Roger tucked in as they talked about the trivial things of the day. Janet looked tired, he thought, and when tired she almost looked her age. There was a remoteness about her which Roger had noticed recently, as if she found it difficult to think about what they were saying, and everything she said came off the surface of her mind. The only real warmth in her voice came when she talked of the boys.

'I feel so tired,' she said about ten o'clock. 'I think I'll have an early night, darling.'

Roger thought: I'm out night after night, and here's one when I'm home and she feels too tired to stay up. It was not a very deep reflection, and when she had gone upstairs he put it out of his mind. He took her some tea and they had it together. By eleven o'clock Janet was dozing off; Roger felt sure that she was asleep almost before he closed the door. She must be tired out. He hoped Hardy wouldn't telephone too soon, and disturb her; and he hoped Hardy wouldn't telephone too late; that would break right across her sleep. It was one of those nights when anyone from the Yard or any hopeful newspaperman might call.

He looked through the documents in his briefcase, making sure that every case he had been working on was annotated so that whoever took it over would have the full picture. This took him until half past eleven. The boys weren't in; next thing he knew, they would telephone to say they would be late.

In fact they arrived just after midnight, big-eyed with the kind of tiredness which youth would never admit. As always Richard had coasted the MG the last fifty yards, and they came in, closing the back door quietly.

'Mum gone to bed?' asked Richard.

'Yes. Does she usually go so early?'

'Most nights,' answered Scoop, and added in one of his devastating moments of frankness: 'After all she would only get bored, sitting up and waiting for you. I say, Dad, what happened at Cannon Row this morning? The newspapers say you tried to save the man who was shot.'

'The newspapers which say that are simply guessing,' Roger declared. 'I didn't have any warning, and I don't think anyone would have been able to save him. Did your mother say much about it?'

'Just read the story in the *Evening News*, but didn't say a word,' Martin answered. He usually arrived back from the College of Art before Richard came in from the studio, and was always better informed about events at home.

'Had any luck?' asked Richard. He was opening the refrigerator door and taking out milk and a chunk of the porkpie. 'I mean, made any more arrests?'

'Not just yet,' Roger said drily.

He left them, went into the front room, poured himself a whisky and soda, and looked through the morning and evening newspapers. The boys poked their heads in, whispered goodnight, and went upstairs; a door banged. There was no creaking sound from Janet above his head, and as he sat back in the easy-chair Roger wished he could go up to bed. He was more than tired enough, but if he was in bed and Hardy telephoned it was bound to wake Janet. Here, the telephone was at his side. He folded up the newspapers, and picked up the skeleton plans, checking how much he knew by heart. As he did so, the telephone bell rang; he snatched the receiver off almost before it had finished its first ring.

'West.'

'You asked me to call you,' Hardy said.

'Sorry to worry you,' said Roger. 'Something's cropped up you ought to know about.' He told the Assistant Commissioner exactly what had happened, and also told him of Soames's reaction, and of what he, Roger, had done.

'Better release the story generally,' decided Hardy. 'I'll talk to Sharp tonight. He can cable Pretoria and tell them what we're going to do and then we can tell the Back-Room Inspector to release it here.'

'Sure you wouldn't like me to do that?'

'Yes, I'm sure.' After a pause, Hardy went on: 'When can you be ready to go?'

Roger's heart began to thump.

'Go where?'

'You know where. The quicker you can see Nightingale and find out what he's really up to, the better. He probably won't talk to the South African police. If he won't talk to you we'll know he's deep in the smuggling,' guessed Hardy. 'Haven't you checked what flights there are to Johannesburg tomorrow?'

'No,' said Roger.

'You're slipping,' Hardy said. 'Why don't you check with London Airport, and then tell Sharp to get you fixed up?'

15

FLIGHT

'WOULD YOU like to come to the airport?' Roger asked Janet. In the past she had been to see him off on long trips abroad, and had always given him the impression that she liked to. This morning, he wasn't sure what her reaction would be. He had told her what Hardy wanted him to do, that there was a BOAC flight to Johannesburg direct at one-thirty that afternoon, which meant that he would be able to spend all the morning at the Yard. When Janet didn't answer now, he went on almost awkwardly: 'Jan, what's the matter?'

'Nothing's the matter.'

'I have to go, you know.'

'I know.'

'Are you coming to see me off?'

'If you want me to.'

Her eyes were lack-lustre where they should be so bright, her manner was almost listless where it was usually brisk and lively. He did not know what to do or say, but he did know that they were expecting him at the Yard and every minute he could spend there would be precious.

'Will you pack a few things for me? I'll call for you at half past twelve,' he said. He wished there was time to suggest that he should come home earlier so that they could have lunch at the airport, but if he promised that and something cropped up to prevent it she would be disappointed. It was better not to risk it. 'How does that sound?'

Janet hesitated; and then she forced a smile and put some enthusiasm into her voice.

'That sounds fine! Now you'd better be off, or you'll be late. You'll need every minute you can squeeze in this morning.' She gave him a peck of a kiss, and shooed him off, but there was something not quite normal about it; she had to make the special effort. He was preoccupied as he drove to the Yard, and whenever he tried to make himself think of the smuggling case, uncertainty about Janet drew his thoughts back to her. Now that he had noticed this remoteness, he realized that it had been gradually developing for some time – certainly for months. And it was a fact that he had spent more and more time at the office in the evening, doing paper-work which never seemed to end, so that he could carry out the actual work of investigation during the day. It had become a habit, he was so deeply involved in his job; could one say that he was obsessed by it?

He turned into the Yard, to find Gorlay waiting, obviously to look after the car.

'Everything all right?' Roger asked.

'Nothing new as far as I know,' said Gorlay. 'Mr Klemm and Mr McKay have been in since seven, to get everything ready before you go.'

Roger said, startled: 'How do they know I'm going anywhere?'

Gorlay grinned: 'Little bird I suppose, sir!'

Roger laughed, and hurried up the steps. There seemed a greater briskness about most of the people whom he saw on the way. He reached his own office to find everything cleared from his desk except the papers and reports on the smuggling investigation, and also to find a clearly-marked list of everything that had been done, and every letter posted, last night. He smiled with satisfaction as he rang for Klemm and McKay, who came in together so quickly that it was obvious that they had been waiting for the summons. Klemm looked bright-eyed, McKay a little tired, but Yard men were used to working through the night and snatching sleep whenever they could.

'Anything new?' Roger asked.

'One thing,' answered Klemm. 'We've had a visit from a taxi-driver – the chap who delivered Van der Lunn to the Common View Hotel. He says that someone paid him a couple of pounds to take the man there, and told him that

Van der Lunn was drunk. Most cabbies get that kind of job. He didn't think anything of it until he saw the description of the motor-scooterist who drove Bradshaw's murderer away.'

Roger asked sharply: 'Same man?'

'The cabby says so.'

'Where'd he pick the passenger up?'

'At the corner of Great Compton Street and Frith Street, but we had a bit of luck.' Klemm looked almost smug. 'The cabby had been round the block, looking for a fare, and had noticed the Italian and the so-called drunk leaving the Seven Seas strip club. He'd seen the Italian before, and swears it was Severini or Galli. The description fits either of them.'

Roger said: 'Better double the watch on that club, though; the manager might know more than he admits.'

'We'll look after this end,' Klemm assured him confidently, and McKay chimed in with a subdued, 'Aye.' Then Klemm went on: 'I've talked to our man at the hospital. Van der Lunn hasn't come round enough to speak yet, and the surgeon says that with the dope they've pumped into him it will certainly be forty-eight hours, and probably a week, before he can tell us anything.'

'What we need is another break,' Roger said. 'You heard about Nightingale?'

'Jameson told us. Bloody fool to go in with a faked passport,' said Klemm. 'Any idea why he did it?'

'I hope to find out tomorrow,' said Roger. 'Now, let's go over the drill for while I'm away. I'll need a detailed report by cable or telephone once a day – find out from Jameson or someone at the South Africa Embassy the best time to get through to Johannesburg. I'd like cabled confirmation on all the salient points and an airmail letter with more details every day. Start telephoning the European police tomorrow. And as the replies come in from our questionnaire, I'd like copies by airmail with word by telephone if you think it's urgent enough. All clear?'

'No trouble,' said Klemm.

'Wouldn't be a bad idea to work from this office while I'm

gone, but you'll be out on your necks the moment I'm back.'
They laughed. 'Anything in about David Bradshaw?'

'All the reports we've had from people who knew him pretty well corroborate the story from Common View Hotel,' answered McKay. 'Except for one thing.'

'What thing?'

'He liked leg and strip shows. Some of the places he visited on flights were very spicy and expensive, from Cairo to Istanbul and Singapore to Hong Kong. There isna' much doubt that the man had exotic and expensive tastes, and the Seven Seas Club was the kind of place he could get what he wanted.'

Roger said softly: 'Let's go.'

.   .   .

The manager was tall, lean, hungry-looking; his secretary somewhat like a Sunday-school teacher who had lost her faith. They were in a small, messy office behind the main room of the club, where the chairs were standing on the tables, cleaners went about their work sluggishly, a Negro barman was busy polishing glasses and dusting bottles. A band of three middle-aged men and a youthful one were rehearsing a new number on the little stage, and the booming of the drum was very loud even in the office. Boom ... Boom ... Boom ... Boom ...

Roger thrust photographs of Nightingale and Van der Lunn in front of the manager and the woman.

'Yes, we were shown those last night, and we've made investigations,' the hungry-looking manager said hurriedly. 'They were here on Monday night, both of them. So was the man I was asked about yesterday, the man with the big nose.'

'David Bradshaw,' Roger said.

'Yes, sir. We recognized him from his photograph. What a terrible thing to happen! And in a police-station!' The man seemed too nervous and edgy to mean that maliciously. 'He was often here, sir. He spent a lot of money, he really was a big spender. But that other man, he didn't spend much.' He pointed to Nightingale's photograph. 'He has been here several times, and I can tell you this, he was usually here when Brad – *Brad*shaw was. No, he didn't spend much, but Bradshaw spent hundreds of pounds some evenings ...'

•   •   •

'What we want is a team to visit banks in the West End area to find out if Bradshaw had accounts with them under different names,' Roger decided. 'And if we can't get any results from the West End, spread the inquiries farther. At the hotel he didn't look as if he had two pennies to rub together, but if he spent money like water at the Seven Seas, he got it from somewhere and maybe he keeps it safely in a bank.'

'We'll fix it,' Klemm promised. His eyes were very bright. 'My God, what a case this is!'

•   •   •

When Roger returned to his office, he found an envelope marked BOAC on the desk. Inside was his return ticket, the return date open, labels, some brochures about South Africa including the game parks, embarkation instructions, and 'Notes of Interest to Passengers'. There was also a note from Hardy, wishing him luck; Hardy was at the Police Conference in the City.

It was a little after twelve o'clock when BOAC telephoned.

'The flight has been put back by one hour, sir. If you care to reach the airport at two-thirty instead of one-thirty that will be in ample time.'

'Ah,' said Roger. 'Thanks.' He put in a call to Janet immediately, and when she answered he spoke with a lilt in his voice which he hoped would bring back an answering response. 'Hallo, sweet! The flight's been put back an hour; we've time to lunch together at the airport restaurant. How about it?'

He was half afraid that she would make some excuse.

'Oh, that's wonderful!' Janet exclaimed.

•   •   •

There was still a hint of remoteness when they had lunch

together. She had packed everything Roger needed, done everything she could, yet she was holding something back. There was a kind of constraint between them even when they said goodbye. Roger had the impression there was something she wanted to say, but could not bring herself to say it.

Hammerton and Jameson were there to see him off at the aircraft itself, and the last face Roger saw out of the window was that of the Negro, smiling his almost-wistful smile.

* * *

Roger found the fascination of the sun glistening on the snow-clad Alps, the beauty of the valleys, the smallness of the towns and villages, the vivid blue of the Mediterranean, as great as ever. The flight over the Mediterranean was so uneventful that it was almost humdrum, but when the mosques and towers of Cairo loomed up, and the fantastic labyrinth of tiny streets slashed here and there by great boulevards, there was a surge of excitement. But they landed too soon. A few passengers got off, two Egyptians and a big Rhodesian got on. They were off in an hour, catching a glimpse of the Nile with its green strips of land on either side, before darkness fell, and the sky was filled with stars of unbelievable brilliance. Roger dozed, had a whisky-and-soda, chatted with a middle-aged passenger across the gangway, ordered a mixed grill, and was waited on as attentively as any VIP. From time to time he glanced through the booklet, which described the land over which they were flying. Down there, hidden by the night, was the Valley of the Nile, the Valley of Kings, the magnificence of Luxor, and the sand of the unending desert.

He dozed off.

When he woke, the stewardess was shaking his shoulder.

'Some tea, sir, we'll soon be at Nairobi.' As he sat up, she added: 'Mount Kenya's looking magnificent this morning.'

The sun, rising out of the dark earth into a clear, pale sky shone on the snow-capped peak, giving it a breathtaking beauty.

There was the usual tension as they went down at Nairobi,

the release from it as the aircraft stopped, then the bustle of passengers getting out and others getting on. Out of Nairobi, they flew over scrub, then over thick jungle, soon over a rock-strewn land. The great Rift Valley looked as if it was something in a relief map, not part of the earth.

The two stewards were younger men than Bradshaw, attentive and pleasant; one of the three stewardesses reminded Roger slightly of Faith Soames.

After breakfast, he tried to think only of the problem ahead. He did not know Nightingale well, but knew him for a strong-willed individual with a one-track mind, or what Soames believed was a one-track mind, for his job. Roger made himself go over everything that had happened and the reports he had read, checking and rechecking, until he felt sure that he knew all the salient points, and was not likely to need to refresh himself with his papers. Once convinced of that, he was able to relax enough to study the passenger's booklet, in which were details of the countries they were flying over, the names of tribes, the kinds of wild animals, and the minerals being mined. Kilimanjaro stood out among the mountains of Kenya, the most breathtaking sight they had seen since Switzerland.

The steward and the stewardesses kept pointing out places of interest in the browny-yellow countryside. For the most part it was broken by ranges of hills, wild and desolate, and twice crossed by great rivers. There was a stirring of excitement when someone exclaimed: 'Look, Kariba!' Suddenly everyone was craning his neck to look out of the tiny windows.

The stewardess who looked like Faith stopped by Roger, and his middle-aged neighbour.

'You'll soon get a good view of it,' she said.

On the north side there was a great sheet of water where the river was dammed, on the south only a trickle. The great wall of the dam was so massive that it was almost as impressive as the Zambesi itself.

Then suddenly, the dam was behind them, and scrub-covered countryside stretched out below, horizon to horizon, trees with tiny leaves that seemed to be only brown or yellow, or the stripped branches of bushes, here and there a huge baobab tree jutting out with its rock-like trunk and its pathetic, stunted limbs.

The middle-aged man said suddenly: 'There's the Limpopo. Now we won't be long. Sluggish-looking stretch of mud, isn't it?'

Very soon they were flying over the hills of Northern Transvaal, seeing mine dumps dotted about everywhere. 'Gold, copper, platinum, and uranium among others,' said the booklet.

Soon they could see Pretoria with its wide streets and tall modern buildings and the stark solidness of the Voortrekker Monument, memorial to the pioneers who had opened up this great land in their search for freedom from British domination. Almost at once the skyscrapers of Johannesburg appeared, and beyond there seemed yellow hills, the slag heaps of the gold-mines, drab and unromantic from the air.

All these things Roger had learned in his youth, and had read about countless times. He had refreshed his memory about most of them on the aircraft, and everything he saw seemed to have its special interest and significance.

'Fasten your belts, please.' The stewardesses called out, then checked each belt. The light showed outside the cockpit, and the *No Smoking* order was flashed on. Routine. Roger saw the flat ground as it appeared to rise up to meet the aircraft, had a familiar moment of anxiety, then felt the gentle bump, another and another; and they were down.

The stewardess who had been so solicitous came up.

'You're to go off first, Mr West. I hope you enjoyed your journey.'

'Very much,' said Roger. He got out of his seat and smiled at her. 'Thanks largely to you.' She looked pleased. The pilot came hurrying from the door which had been closed most of the flight, and reached the head of the steps just behind Roger.

'Glad to have met you, Superintendent – always good to have celebrities aboard.'

Roger chuckled as he shook hands.

'I don't know what the blarney is about, but thanks.' He started down the steps and saw two men moving towards him from a dark-blue Chevrolet with a coloured chauffeur standing by it. Both were in a pale-brown uniform which looked as if it were made of linen or drill; he thought at first that they were soldiers, then remembered that the South African police wore uniforms like this.

They drew up, and the elder of the two, in his fifties, shook hands.

'Superintendent West?'

'Yes.'

'I am Colonel Wiess. This is Captain Standish. We are very glad to make your acquaintance and grateful that you have come so promptly.'

Both men had powerful handshakes. Wiess spoke rather like du Toit, but with a harder voice; Standish had an ordinary English voice with a slight twang in it; he had a broad, very tanned face and his blue eyes had the bright clarity of periwinkles. Wiess was rather more florid, rather more fleshy.

Wiess was saying: 'We have heard much about you, of course, even before this investigation. We hope you will call on us for anything you need while you are in South Africa.'

'I certainly will,' said Roger.

They whisked him through Customs. A boy wearing a khaki shirt and khaki shorts carried his two bags, and would have taken his briefcase had he not held on to it. His first impression was of a vast, vivid blue sky, and of a heat which seemed to strike at him. The shade of the Customs house had been welcome. Now he stepped out of that shade into the open air outside the shed, and walked towards the car only a short distance away. The driver stood at attention, smart in a closed-neck jacket and a topee, which was a cross between khaki and grey. He opened the doors. The officers got in the back, where there was plenty of room for all three. The driver drove off smoothly.

'We are at the Jan Smuts International Airport,' Wiess said. 'It serves both Johannesburg, to the south, and Pretoria, to the north. We shall be in Pretoria in about half an hour.'

At some cross-roads, a Bantu constable on point duty held up a low-lying red sports car to allow them to pass. Only as they turned to the right, away from the sports car, did Roger see the driver.

It was Faith Soames.

16

REMINDER

ROGER SAW Faith smiling, as if she was mocking him; and then she disappeared. Wiess looked at him questioningly, and Standish, who had been on the side near the girl, raised one eyebrow, as if to say: 'We have a ladies' man.' Neither South African spoke. A few cars and some trucks passed them. Perhaps it was because there were so many Jamaicans in London, but the fact that there were so many dark skins here was hardly noticeable.

'If you will tell us what you would like to do first,' Wiess said, 'we will arrange it. Let me say at once that we placed James Nightingale under arrest with the greatest reluctance and only when we were sure that the evidence was very strong. We do not wish to arouse the antagonism of any section of the British Press for the sake of it.'

'I know what you mean,' said Roger. 'Did you see the girl in the red Jaguar?'

'No,' said Wiess.

'Yes,' said Standish.

'She's here from *The Globe*,' Roger told them. 'I saw her in London the evening before last, so she must have caught a plane that night. *The Globe* isn't losing much time.' He told them more about Faith and more about Nightingale, and added: 'If Soames is sure that this is a justifiable charge, he won't try to be spiteful. All he wants is what we want –

the truth.' He felt almost pompous as he uttered the words, but neither of the others appeared to notice it. 'How much hotter does it get?' he inquired.

'This is not what we consider a hot day,' said Wiess. 'And when you are a little more used to it I do not believe that you will find it unpleasant. You were going to tell me what you would like to do first.'

Roger thought: He's not going to waste any time, either. He had a feeling that Standish was watching him more critically than Wiess was. It would be easy to say he would like a general picture of the situation first, but probably better if he had a specific request. He could see Nightingale almost at once, and let Wiess have a copy of all the details of the Klemm–McKay plan. They were both waiting on him.

'I'd like a thorough briefing on the case against Nightingale, and then I'd like to see him. If he's involved in the smuggling, we can get a lead through him, if he isn't we have to try and find out what's been happening. He may have some information that would help us.'

'If you can believe what he says,' said Standish.

'You don't believe him, do you?'

'No,' said Standish.

'Captain Standish does not want to allow the benefit of the doubt,' said Wiess. 'I think we have to accept the possibility that Nightingale is innocent of any major crime although undoubtedly guilty of breaking some of our laws.'

'Using a false passport would get him in trouble at any frontier,' Roger said. 'Who's in charge of the case against him?'

'I am, under Colonel Wiess,' answered Standish.

'And I am in charge of investigations into the diamond smuggling,' Wiess said. 'I am sure you are right, you should deal with Nightingale first, and we should go on from there. Superintendent, would you prefer to be the private guest of a senior officer, or would you prefer to be in a hotel?'

'A hotel, I think,' Roger said, half apologetically.

Standish gave a twisted kind of smile. Roger wished that he had taken to the man, and wondered if Standish had any bee in his bonnet or had any sense of grievance against the Yard. There was certainly something in his manner which Roger did not like.

'We have provisionally reserved a suite for you at the New Pretoria Hotel,' said Wiess. 'It is close to our new Police Headquarters, and convenient for the centre of the city. We have arranged for you to be able to call on a secretary, and if you need personal assistants Captain Standish will arrange whatever is necessary. Will you forgive me if I ask one favour?'

'Of course,' Roger said mechanically.

'Our ways and our methods are not always the same as yours, and I will be grateful if you do not take any course of action without first consulting Captain Standish or me. It is not that I believe you would do so without good reason, but it could give rise to misunderstanding and it could also cause delays and possibly cause harm.' Wiess was looking straight at Roger as he spoke, matter-of-fact in manner and yet obviously determined that he should be taken seriously.

'Colonel,' Roger said with equal bluntness, 'I shan't throw my weight about.'

Before Wiess could comment or Standish react in any way, there was a red flash on the road, and the scarlet Jaguar passed them on the wide dual carriageway; it must have been travelling at ninety miles an hour. Faith was driving with that kind of self-confidence given to few women, but when given, as effective as any man's. She disappeared round a curve.

Soon they were in the outskirts of the city, driving along a tree-lined road with good-class houses on either side. They passed a number of garages and beneath an underpass; then they seemed to be in the middle of a bustling, thriving metropolis.

Five minutes later, Roger was in his hotel.

The manager was present to receive the party. Three white-clad boys stood in attendance. Signing in was quite a ceremony. There were a few formal words of welcome, and then they went up in a lift which might have been in the hotel of any American city. The place was streamlined and ultramodern, the passages very wide, and the muted strains of piped music made a pleasant background of sound. The manager unlocked the door of Number 505, near the lift, and led the way into a large room furnished in contemporary style, with grey venetian blinds at the enormously wide window. There were two telephones, two desks, all the comfort he could imagine – there was even a dictaphone.

'I shall leave a sergeant downstairs and he will bring you to Police Headquarters whenever you are ready. We shall have Nightingale there,' Wiess added. 'If you require anything, please ring the bell or telephone.'

'*Anything*,' Standish echoed, and there seemed to be a suggestive note in his voice.

They went out; and almost as soon as the door closed there was a tap at it. A boy whose dark face and arms showed jet black against his snow-white jacket and short trousers, stood there holding a tea-tray.

'For you, baas,' he said, and smiled almost enough to split his face in two.

'That's just what I wanted,' Roger said. 'Put it on the table.' There was a long coffee-table by the window. 'Can you pull up those blinds?'

'Sure thing, baas.' The boy went across and drew them up without effort, locked them by pulling the cord diagonally away from the top, then moved away. 'I am your special room-boy, baas. Anything you want, just send for me. I will be in the passage, always ready.'

'What's your name?' asked Roger.

'Percival, baas.'

Percival went out, closing the door quietly. Roger looked out on to the wide street. Opposite there was another high, modern building with the word *Volksbank* on it, and some magnificent statuary of animals at the massive front steps. The rest of the buildings in sight seemed old-fashioned. The pavements were crowded, but motor traffic was not very dense.

Roger turned away and opened the file which Wiess had given him about Nightingale, poured out tea, and began to read and to drink. He had been there for five minutes, already half forgetting the journey, when there was another tap at the door. He called:

'Come in.'

Once again it was Percival, still beaming all over his face, perhaps more nervous than he appeared to be. He carried a silver dish with half a dozen cream *éclairs* on it, brought them in swinging a silver handle, and declared:

'I'm very sorry, baas, I forgot the very nice cakes.' He put them down, backed away and went out.

Roger finished his first cup of tea, looked at the tempting cakes, and then noticed a small envelope underneath one of them. He picked this up. It was plain, probably a goodwill message from the police or the hotel, he imagined, and opened it. Inside was a single fold of paper, and on it a single question: *Who do the cakes remind you of?*

So Faith Soames was in the hotel, already casting her spell over the staff.

•   •   •

Roger had a shave and a shower, changed into a light-weight pale-brown suit which he had worn when he had been to Australia in the summer, and felt fresh and ready to tackle even Standish and Nightingale when he went out. Percival had already taken out the tray. No one had called him, although he would not have been surprised to have a call from the newspapers. He moved slowly into the carpeted stealth of the passages, and pressed the bell for the lift. It was automatic, but a boy in a puce-coloured uniform and wearing a white fez-type cap was in attendance; he also wore enormous white gloves. In the foyer, a Bantu police-sergeant in starch-stiffened uniform, buttoned up jacket and topee like the driver's, came towards him and saluted.

'I am Sergeant Horo, sir. You wish to visit the Police Headquarters now?'

'Yes, please.'

'You go by car, sir, or you walk?'

'I'll walk,' decided Roger.

They left the hotel, waited by some traffic lights with a crowd of white people and coloured people who seemed as

123

oblivious of one another as in any crowd, and went across on the green, passed rows of parked cars and windows crammed with goods, turned a corner and then another corner and came upon the Police Headquarters, a long, low modern building. Police were on duty outside, as they would be at the Yard. The reception office had obviously been warned to expect him, and Horo led the way up one flight of stairs and then along to a room with *Colonel Wiess* printed in black on the door. The sergeant tapped, turned the handle, stood aside, saluted, and announced:

'Superintendent West, Colonel.'

Wiess was alone, and Roger had the impression that he was more preoccupied than he had been in the car. He shrugged his preoccupation off, however, pointed to a chair, and said:

'I have read your report closely, Superintendent, and there is nothing about it with which I disagree. You make me feel almost hopeful of reaching a solution before long. Before you see Nightingale, I would like to make a few remarks.'

'Of course,' Roger said.

'There is some apparent connection between Mr Van der Lunn's movements and Nightingale's, and it is clear that you do not regard them as coincidental. I confess I hope they are, but I agree that they may not be. Mr Van der Lunn has the confidence of the Government, and I find it almost impossible to believe that he would act at any time contrary to the Government's interest. I should perhaps say the country's interest. Have you any reason to believe that I am wrong?'

'Not yet,' Roger said. 'I don't know how big the job is, but I can't see a man in Van der Lunn's position finding it worth it.'

'I am glad you feel like that,' said Wiess. 'It is not possible to value the amount involved for certain. It is a large sum, but not large by Van der Lunn's standards.'

'How large?' inquired Roger.

'We have been asked forty-one times for proof that packets of diamonds shipped from this country actually left. In each case, we can offer proof that the diamonds were inspected visually by our Customs officers. The average value of each packet was twenty thousand rands.'

Startled, Roger said: 'Twenty thousand rands equals ten thousand pounds sterling. That's a lot of money.'

'It is indeed.' After a pause, Wiess went on: 'Now that you have studied the reports on Nightingale – are you satisfied with what followed?'

'If I'd been in your position I would have held him,' Roger said flatly. 'What about those diamonds?'

'It is possible that he is telling the truth, and they were put in his luggage,' answered Wiess.

'So he isn't proved guilty of anything more than illegal entry.'

'In this country that is a more serious offence than it might be in others, but I seem to remember certain incidents where you have received illegal immigrants and refused to allow them to stay.' There was no smile and no edge to his voice as he said that. 'I think we shall have to be convinced very strongly that Mr Nightingale's presence is in the country's interests. But I keep an open mind. He is now downstairs, in a cell. Would you prefer to see him there, or would you like him to be in a waiting-room?'

'I'll see him in the cell,' Roger decided.

17

NIGHTINGALE

ROGER HAD forgotten that Nightingale was so tall; an inch taller than he, Roger, which made him six foot two or three. He was broad but spare; if anything, too thin. His cheeks were slightly hollow, while his square chin was very bony. He had close-cropped brown hair, with plenty of peppering and salting; an older man than Roger had thought, too, certainly in his middle forties. Because of the leanness of his features he had a rather gaunt look, but that was relieved by the mobility of his lips and the brightness of his fine grey eyes, with clearly-defined eyebrows and long lashes. There was something very striking about him, and the word which sprang to Roger's mind was 'buccaneering'. Piratical, in fact; and the way he had blustered into South Africa with the false passport suggested that his temperament matched his appearance. Piratical, Roger thought again: the classic smuggler. Did this impression affect Wiess or Standish in their attitudes?

The cell was much more modern than any at Scotland Yard or Cannon Row; shiny with fresh paint, quite comfortable with a padded seat-chair and a single bed, a washbasin, a partitioned-off WC. Nightingale was facing the door of the cell as the lieutenant-in-charge of cells unlocked it. Two other policemen were at hand, and these men were armed. Roger remembered what had happened to David Bradshaw when he had visited him in his cell. He shivered.

Nightingale, who had been sitting on the bed reading a heavy book, still held it. It had a red, white, and blue cover. He watched while the door was opened and Roger stepped inside, but he didn't move back, which meant that they had to stand close together.

The door clanged behind them, and keys jangled.

'So the Yard sent its glamour boy,' Nightingale jeered. 'I'm flattered.'

'You don't have to think about being flattered. You have to wonder how long you're going to spend behind bars,' Roger said sharply.

'You, too?' That was a sneer.

'Me, too, what?'

'Like these gentry, presume me guilty in the hope that I can never prove my innocence.'

'You can't prove you didn't have a false passport.'

'Oh, that.' Nightingale shrugged. 'You can't even begin to know the problems of a newspaperman – there's always some flare-up where they crack down on the Press, hold 'em at frontiers and airports. So I have a spare one.' He grinned fiercely. 'I didn't think the South African Government would want me around, but I should have known I'd be recognized.

I was in a hurry, so I took a chance. When are you going to get me out?'

'You can get one thing clear from the start,' Roger said. 'I'm not here to look after your interests, that's up to Soames and your newspaper. I'm here to find out whether you can help us solve a series of serious crimes which now includes murder and kidnapping. If you co-operate it should make your own lawyer's task easier. If you're stubborn or awkward you'll make it worse, because already you look as guilty as hell.'

Nightingale backed a pace.

'You're a straightforward bastard, anyhow.' His tone changed only a little. He threw the book on to the bed and it fell so that when Roger glanced at it the title was easy to read: *A Start in Freedom*, by Sir Hugh Foot. Somehow it seemed logical that Nightingale should read a book about colour and race problems in his present predicament: it was a form of defiance. 'What kind of confession do you want?'

'Full, free, and fast,' said Roger. He moved to the bed and sat down; he was feeling irritated by this man, and Standish had already put him on edge. 'I've been through all the statements you've made, all the statements made by everyone at the Customs office, and by the police after they questioned you and searched your luggage. They say you were present when the bag of industrial diamonds was found – were you?'

'Yes.'

'And you hadn't seen it before?'

'That's what my statement says.'

'Try telling me,' Roger said. He leaned back against the wall, narrowing his eyes, but soon wished he hadn't sat down because in a way it put him at a disadvantage. 'We probably speak the same kind of language. Did you know the diamonds were in your baggage?'

'I did not.'

'Have you any idea who put them there?'

'Some Customs bastard, probably.'

Roger said, quietly, firmly: 'Now you know as well as I do

that you're talking nonsense. Go on like it, and I'll have to regard you as hostile and a suspect. I don't want to think one of Britain's best newspaper correspondents is a criminal, but after your passport trick, I'm prepared to believe it possible.' When Nightingale didn't answer, Roger repeated: 'Have you any idea who put the bag of diamonds in your baggage?'

'No.'

'Had you ever seen it before?'

'No.'

'When had you last been through your baggage?'

'In London – and it wasn't there then. Take it from me, Handsome, that bag of diamond dust was put in at London Airport or while it was on the aircraft or here in Pretoria.'

'Or at Nairobi – didn't you land there?'

Nightingale frowned. 'Or at Nairobi,' he agreed. 'Don't let's forget any place.'

'If you forget anything that could help clear you, don't expect anyone else to remember it for you. Have you ever used a false passport before to enter South Africa?'

'No,' said Nightingale; he gave the impression that he hadn't expected that question.

'How often have you been to South Africa?'

'Half a dozen times.'

'When were the others?'

'In nineteen-sixty, first. Once during the Sharpeville trouble, twice over the Mandela treason trials, and three or four times over this business.'

'On your genuine passport?'

'Yes. Your memory isn't so good, is it?' Nightingale's lips twisted sardonically.

'As a matter of fact my memory is better than average and I've spent a lot of time in the last twenty-four hours taking a refresher course on the questions I'm asking you. And there are a lot of things I remember which I don't like about the situation. The last time I questioned a man in a police-cell, for instance, he was shot dead in front of my eyes.'

There was no doubt about Nightingale's reaction to that; he was astounded. He backed a pace, knocked against a chair, and then slowly lowered himself to it. His eyes were first very rounded, rather like Scoop's, and then slowly narrowed, as the truth began to seep into his mind. Before he spoke he put his hand to his pocket and drew out a packet of cigarettes; so the police were not making things too difficult for him. He took out a book of matches, too, and lit a cigarette.

'Who?' he asked.

'An acquaintance of yours.'

'Who?'

'David Bradshaw.'

Nightingale's eyes closed spasmodically, and he seemed to wince; then he kept them closed for what seemed a long time, opened them slowly, and said:

'So you know we knew each other.'

'I know you sometimes stayed at the Common View Hotel as Knight; I know you were taken to be some kind of sales representative; I know you spent a lot of time with Bradshaw at the Seven Seas Club. In fact, you'd be surprised how much I know about you – where you've been, where you've reported from, most things that Soames could tell me or I could find out for myself.'

'Who shot Bradshaw?'

'A man about five feet in height who wore Italian-style clothes and shoes, had a small nose with broad nostrils, black hair which grew low-down on his forehead, eyes so brown they looked black – who is he?'

Nightingale said slowly: 'I can tell you one thing about him.'

Roger felt the first surge of excitement and real hope. He believed that the newspaper correspondent was now telling the truth, that if he went on doing that he might really give some information which mattered. Roger did not prompt him. Outside, out of sight, a man walked up and down the passage; he smothered a cough.

'Bradshaw used to see this man at the Seven Seas,' Nightingale went on slowly. 'I cottoned on to Bradshaw when I was at London Airport one evening – I saw him slip a packet into a porter's pocket. He collected it from the porter after he'd been through Customs. So I followed him. He went to the Seven Seas, and left the packet at the cloakroom. Later, the Italian collected it.' Nightingale paused, then continued with a smile which made his lips go very thin : 'The same gent used to try to sell me obscene books and photographs. I wasn't in the market.'

'Do you know the man's name, what he was doing at the Seven Seas, whether he was employed there or just a customer?' Roger rapped the questions out.

'I don't know his name. He was selling smut, but I don't know what else. Women, probably. I don't think he was employed or a customer. He used to go round to a lot of Soho's nightclubs. They let him in just as Continental restaurants allow newspaper sellers in.'

Roger said : 'I can believe that, anyhow.' He took a notebook from his pocket, scribbled, and went to the bars and called : 'Excuse me.' The lieutenant-in-charge came hurrying briskly, keys at the ready. 'I wonder if you would ask Captain Standish or Colonel Wiess to get that cable off at once,' he said, passing the note through the bars. 'I'll be some time yet.'

'Very good, Superintendent.'

'Thanks.' Roger moved back to Nightingale, who was beginning to smile again, although he made no comment. Roger dropped down on to the bed. 'I've told the Yard to do the rounds of the Soho strip clubs including the Seven Seas for that man,' he said. 'Did Soames know about your use of a faked passport?'

Nightingale grinned, and said : 'The prisoner refused to answer on the grounds that he might incriminate his employer.' When Roger glared at him, he went on : 'Pack it in, Handsome. It's been done a thousand times. Maybe it's a nominal offence, but it isn't as if I've ever used a faked passport when I didn't have a genuine one tucked away in case of emergency.'

'What happened to your real passport this time?'

'It was stolen – presumably at the time that the diamond packet was put in my baggage. By now the great detective ought to realize that someone has been framing the distinguished newspaper correspondent. That's what happened. I came here to get a story, a big story, and I did it the way I thought best. I didn't come to consort with criminals, or smuggle diamonds, or conflict with the coppers, or to write a story about the wicked Nats. Just in case you're in any doubt I don't share all Soames's political prejudices or opinions. I'm a bit *anti* civil rights if anything. I don't think a man's my equal simply because his skin's black – or yellow or white, for that matter.'

'Why come here for the story? Why not stay in London?'

'It was born here, its heart is here, and it will be solved from here.'

'Is Van der Lunn at the centre of it?'

For the second time, Roger's question caught Nightingale off his balance, and the newspaperman showed his surprise so unmistakably that there was no point in trying to pretend. He gave a slow smile, as if in reluctant approval of the question.

'It wouldn't surprise me.'

'Why did you telephone Soames about Van der Lunn and then disappear?'

'Now that's a question,' Nightingale said. 'Call it intuition. I didn't want the old man to know that I even suspected Van der Lunn was involved. Once Soames realized that the fat would be in the fire, he'd make all the news capital out of it that he could, and do everything possible to discredit a man known to be one of the non-political Nationalist hierarchy. On the other hand, if I hadn't mentioned Van der Lunn I would have got a rocket and I might even have been sacked. So I gave Soames a hint, and then followed Van der Lunn. I didn't follow him far.'

'Why did you follow him at all?'

'Because Bradshaw was fussing about him like an old hen, and the porter who'd helped Bradshaw smuggle a packet in took Van der Lunn through Customs and out to a private car. I thought it had been sent from the Embassy. My own car was impeded by a motor-scooterist who swerved in front of me and then skidded – I had to find out whether he was injured. Couldn't have trailed them, anyhow; there were too many other cars about. I lost track of Van der Lunn and had to decide what my next move would be pretty quick. I decided to come here and try to find out more about Van der Lunn's activities. While I don't share my boss's liberal prejudices, I do share his passion for a sensational story, and if I could prove that Van der Lunn was tied up in the diamond smuggling this would be one of the biggest. It wasn't any use wasting time looking for him in London, and in any case, the fact that a man on a motor-scooter had side-tracked me might mean that someone was watching me in London – my interest in Van der Lunn was probably known. So I changed to my *alias*, James Knight, and caught a plane out of London the same evening – I phoned *The Globe* from the airport.'

'And Soames didn't know where you were going?'

'No.'

'You talked to your editor, and didn't think it worth reporting that you were going on a six-thousand-mile flight on what might be a wild-goose chase?'

'My editor gives me a job. He doesn't tell me how to do it. He belts me if I fall down on it, but I don't fall down very often.' Nightingale was more relaxed now than he had been since Roger had come into the cell, and he leaned back, folded his arms behind his head, rested his neck on his hands, and went on: 'That's it and all about it. I didn't get a chance of finding out what Van der Lunn gets up to in Pretoria before they caught me. I believe they guessed I'd come because of the Van der Lunn mystery, and decided to make sure I couldn't probe far. All right, all right,' Nightingale added quickly. 'I know they've legal cause. I can't plead illegal detention, but you asked me the question and I'm giving you the answer. They didn't want me to find out any more about Van der Lunn.'

After a pause, Roger said: 'So that's what you think.'

'That's what I think.'

'Let's see how good a writer you are,' said Roger. 'Put all this down on paper. Cross all the t's and dot all the i's. Don't leave anything out, whether it's about Van der Lunn or the Pretoria police, what you think of the Customs, or anything at all. Sign it as a statement. And I'll try to get your release on the strength of it.'

Nightingale said, slowly: 'You'll do that?'

'Yes.'

'I really believe you would,' said Nightingale wonderingly. 'You won't get away with it, but I really believe you'll try. All right. Tell them I want some ruled paper and a ballpoint pen – and some whisky.'

18

FAIR EXCHANGE?

As he walked up from the cells and into the main part of the building, Roger had the same impression he had at New Scotland Yard in the evening and at weekends; that everything was quiet and deserted, the affairs of the law being maintained by a skeleton staff. But Colonel Wiess was in his office, and Standish entered almost on Roger's heels. Wiess was still looking preoccupied, Standish rather tired.

Roger reported, almost *verbatim*.

'... and if he signs this statement, you think that we should take his word for it and allow him to go free,' said Wiess. 'Even if that were what I felt would be the proper course, I could not make sure that it would be done. Illegal entry is a political matter as well as a police one. Certainly there would be delays.'

'You don't see what I'm driving at,' Roger said.

'Just point the way,' put in Standish.

'If Nightingale is released and allowed to move freely about South Africa he'll do one of two things. He'll try to leave the country, and you can stop him again, or he'll try to get his story. I think he'll go for his story. Some newspapermen are dedicated to getting news, and he's one of them. If he tries to investigate Van der Lunn's activities in South Africa, you can keep behind him all the time and stop him at any stage you want. If he's mixed up in the crimes, he can't lead us to any accomplices if he's in prison, but he could if he were released.'

Wiess listened with his head raised, and his chin thrust forward; there was something basilisk about him; even predatory. He stared at Roger for a long time, then shifted his gaze to Standish.

'And what is your opinion, Captain?'

If Wiess takes Standish's advice, I'm sunk, Roger thought. But he did not look at the English-speaking police-officer, only at the Afrikaner.

'I think West has something,' Standish answered, and made Roger look round at him in surprise. 'Nightingale's no use to anyone in a cell. He's only an embarrassment. If we release him but hold his passport, that will be very liberal of us. If he's a crook, he could possibly give himself away. I'd let him go if he signs that statement.'

After another pause, Colonel Wiess said: 'I will have to refer the matter to the Minister of Justice, but I will recommend it. I would not expect to have a decision until late tonight and perhaps tomorrow morning, Mr West. I wish I could ask you to have dinner with me and my wife, but we have a preoccupation.' He half smiled. 'There has been a disturbance between Indians and Bantus near Johannesburg, and the matter is urgent. I can recommend a very good restaurant.'

'And I could do with an early night,' Roger said. 'Will you let Nightingale know that the suggestion is being considered?'

'Yes, I will. And if you would like an escort back to your hotel—'

'I'd like to walk round on my own,' said Roger.

'As you wish. At least allow Captain Standish to recommend the most attractive area and the best arcades,' said Wiess.

Standish walked with Roger to a corner of Church Square, pointing out the most interesting parts of the city centre. He was obviously in a hurry, and something had made him much less sardonic. Roger wondered if the 'disturbance' was, in fact, much more serious than Wiess had made out. He walked past shops which might have been in an English city, but every now and again came upon one which was so different that it could only be in Africa. There were not many people about, and most of the strollers were Bantu. All were in European dress. Most of them looked well-kept and well-nourished. On a corner a mountainous man and a tiny, fragile wife made a chain with three children, all hand-in-hand. Two girls had huge eyes and beautifully-plaited hair tied in red ribbon; the boy's head was a close crop of curls. They were all well-dressed and immaculate. Two middle-aged white women, looking shabby and untidy, looked at the children with obvious approval.

Here and there were big arcades, the shop-windows dressed almost as well as those of Burlington Arcade, and obviously cool even during the noonday heat. Now it was warm but dry and pleasant. Roger crossed where Standish had told him, and found an enormous souvenir-store on a corner, with exquisite carvings of men and animals, drums, shields, spears, lion skins, zebra skins, at the back a magnificent stuffed leopard, against one wall some grotesque witch-doctor masks. Janet could have spent hours there. He spent five minutes and earmarked a tall giraffe with a surprised expression as a possible gift for Janet, and a tribal mask for Scoop; he could see nothing which might appeal to Richard. He strolled back to the hotel. No one followed him, no one showed any interest in him until he neared the lift, when the sergeant who had escorted him to Police Headquarters appeared and saluted but did not speak. Roger said: 'Goodnight,' and went up in the lift. The lift-boy on duty hardly came up to his waist, and was all white teeth. Roger opened the door of his suite and went in, closed the door, and then heard a movement from inside the second room.

Alarm shot through him, touched with fear.

Before he could move, before he could even think, Faith Soames appeared in the communicating doorway.

Roger was taken completely by surprise. Obviously the girl expected him to be, and her smile showed pleasure and satisfaction. She was beautifully groomed. She wore a one-piece dress which seemed to mould her figure, and she was fuller at the bosom than he remembered. She might have been one of the leading models of London, Paris, or New York, standing with one hand on the door frame, the other on her hip, smiling; and no one could have been blamed for calling the smile inscrutable.

Roger said: 'One day you're going to grow up. How did you get in?'

'A good newspaperwoman doesn't allow locks to stop her.'

'A good newspaperman has just allowed a faked passport to stop him, and isn't enjoying the consequences. On the whole I'd say that forcing entry is a worse crime than faking a passport.'

'Are you determined to be beastly?' Faith moved slowly from her pose, and came towards him, her hands raised to her waist, the long, delicate fingers slightly curled, as if she were inviting him to move towards her. The devil of it was, he had to fight against the impulse to go forward, to take her hands, to take her in his arms. Her honey-coloured eyes were bright and glowing, and he had the impression that she knew exactly what effect she was having on him.

'Faith,' he said, 'I don't know what's going on in that mind of yours, but I can tell you some things that aren't.' His mouth was dry. She was still drawing nearer, and he wanted to move back and yet wanted to go forward at the same time; either way would be to acknowledge defeat. 'Do you really want to make the situation worse for Nightingale?'

That stopped her, giving him some cause for satisfaction. The glow faded from her eyes, and her arms fell by her side.

'What do you mean?'

'I mean that whether you forced the lock, or found it open, or bribed the room-boy to let you in, the police know you're here. They're watching you as well as looking after me as their guest. They know who you are and why you're here. If you start breaking their laws, they'll take it for granted that this is a conspiracy between you and Nightingale, probably with the connivance of *The Globe*. Now do you understand why I wonder what's going on in your mind? You couldn't have done a sillier thing.'

She had moved neither backwards nor forwards.

'There's one other way of looking at it,' she said flatly.

'Tell me.'

'I could have come here at your invitation.'

Roger thought: The little bitch. She was beginning to smile again, as if she knew that her comment worried him, and that once again she was in the ascendancy. He wondered whether she was really as ruthless as she tried to make out, and how much of what she said and implied was attempted bluff. The physical attraction which he had felt for her had faded, at least for the time being, and he no longer felt the urge to move forward towards her.

'If they have to choose between believing you or believing me, they won't choose you,' he retorted. He moved for the first time, past her, towards the window. The venetian blinds were down again so no one could see into the room, and he wondered whether they had been lowered by the room-boy or by Faith. 'I'll tell you who could be in serious trouble.'

She had turned round, but didn't step towards him.

'Who?'

'Percival, my room-boy.'

'What makes you so sure I bribed him?'

'I'm not worried if you bribed him; he would take your money and rush to report to his boss. But if you came in when he left the door open, he could be in trouble for falling down on his job.'

'Do you really think that?' She looked perturbed.

'Yes.'

'He came in to lower the blinds, and I slipped in behind him, and hid in the wall-cupboard by the door,' Faith said. 'I'm in Room 501, just along the passage. He certainly doesn't know I'm here.' She frowned. 'He wouldn't get in trouble for something as simple as that, surely.'

Roger said: 'Losing his job could be serious enough trouble for him.' He turned round from the window and sat down on a long contemporary-style settee, all foam rubber, highly-polished wood and black mock-mohair. He crossed his legs and looked up at the girl, completely sure of himself now, temptation firmly in check, policeman and detective fully in control of the man. 'What do you want, anyway?'

She didn't answer.

'Am I supposed to guess?'

'You ought to be able to guess, but you don't have to,' said Faith. Now she began to smile as if she, too, had become more confident of herself. She pulled up a stool which had a thong seat, the thongs criss-crossed in little squares. She sat down on this, and it was impossible not to be aware of the grace of her movements, the fact that she lowered herself as if without effort, and sat without support although the stool was low. She tucked her legs to one side and hugged her knees; the dress slid upwards, so that the nylon-clad legs showed as far up as the double layer of stocking; and above he caught a glimpse of her white skin. Everything about her was posed, and yet at the same time it had a contradictory naturalness.

'All right,' Roger said. 'I won't guess.'

'I came to suggest a fair exchange,' she said.

'Did you?'

'A very fair exchange.' She leaned backwards a little, and her eyes narrowed but they were glowing again, perhaps with the light which came in at the slats of the blinds; it was strange that in leaning backwards while hugging her knees, she gave a remarkable impression of seductiveness. It seemed to Roger that she could turn on that seductiveness at will; that one moment he had seen her simply as a witness and a rather silly young woman, and the next he felt as if all he wanted to do was to go closer to her. Siren-like, she was calling him, inviting him, promising . . .

'An exchange of what?' he asked.

'Roger,' she said, very softly, 'I want to know what Jim Nightingale said, and I know that I won't have a chance to talk to him. I also know you wouldn't lie to me.' She paused, still smiling, still leaning away from him, and affecting him with that almost magnetic attraction. 'So why don't we exchange what you can tell me about Nightingale – just what Jim said, nothing else – for a night of passion?'

19

NIGHT OF PASSION

ROGER FELT quite sure that she meant exactly what she said: that she was offering herself in exchange for information. Yet there was something else, something he only dimly understood, but which seemed to become clearer all the time he looked at her. She was quite beautiful, her skin was flawless, her body feline in its suppleness. Now she leaned farther back, almost as if she would fall off the stool, and her eyes were so narrow that he could hardly see beyond the sweeping lashes. She was smiling, and showing only a glimpse of white teeth. Roger felt an overwhelming temptation to go forward, to stretch out his hands, to draw her towards him; and at the same time he knew that it would be folly and it might be fatal to all prospects of success in the investigation. So he edged farther on to the corner of the couch, looking relaxed – hoping that he looked relaxed – and half smiling.

'Passion,' he echoed. He managed to draw all the fire out of the word, to make it sound flat and lifeless.

'Is it so long since you knew what it was like?' Faith asked.

'You need two minds for passion,' he said.

Her smile widened a little.

'Two bodies, surely.'

'Faith,' Roger said, 'I don't think we're going to agree on what constitutes passion.' He searched for words which might break through her pose of sophisticated sexuality, and said deliberately: 'It's a long time since a nice girl asked me to go to bed with her. I've never seen bed as part of a business deal, though, and I'm not going to start in Pretoria.' He smiled; and he was pleased with the smile, it was brisk and bright and matter-of-fact. 'Supposing we forget that.'

'Handsome,' she said again, 'you might never get another chance like it.'

'I'll take the risk.'

'You've made one mistake for certain,' she said.

'What's that?'

'Thinking I'm a nice girl.'

'A she-devil when roused?' mocked Roger. He shifted his position, sitting more upright; the triumph of mind over body had given him a lot of satisfaction, and he felt that the moment of danger was past. 'The female of the species being more deadly than the male – is that what you mean?'

Faith did not move, hardly seemed to be breathing, just looking at him, and trying to draw him towards her, and smiling in a way he could only think of as inscrutable.

'My uncle always told me that there is a Puritan buried deep in every Englishman, and a Victorian in every father. I'm beginning to see what he meant. Are you really as wife-bound as you're pretending?'

It would be easy to resent the word 'wife-bound'. It would be foolish to show her any sign of resentment. Now he began to think more about Faith as a person rather than about her proposal, and again he wondered what was really going on in her mind.

'Let's say when I get home I'll feel happier if I can look at my wife without hoping she doesn't find out that a sex-kitten in South Africa seduced me.'

'So it's fear of being found out,' Faith retorted. 'What are you really worrying about? We're six thousand miles away from your wife and home. The only people who can possibly know we're in this room together are the police, and they aren't judges of morals – oh, I forgot! Here they are, but we're not in any danger, our skins are both white. Our skins are both white,' she repeated, very softly. 'Beautiful and white. Forget the possibility that someone will find out and betray you, Handsome. Your wife can't believe that a man as virile as you, who has to spend so much time away from her, is so virtuous that he never makes a concession to his manliness.'

'You might know what you believe, but you can't guess what my wife thinks,' Roger retorted. 'Now supposing we stop this nonsense. There are some things I may be able to tell you tomorrow, but I'm not going to say a word tonight. I've had a long day and I'm tired. But I'd like a good dinner before going to bed. Colonel Wiess recommended the Sky Room at the top of a new hotel – would you like to have dinner there with me?'

'And forgiving, too,' Faith said. There seemed a touch of malice in the word, almost as if she was angry and possibly hurt in her pride, but did not want to let him know it. When he looked back on this interlude, he would probably regard it as one of the strangest in his life. He stood up, adding: 'I'm assured that the food's really good.'

She didn't stand up, but leaned a little to one side in order to see him more clearly.

'Handsome,' she said, 'I think you're being very gallant. You needn't be. And you're being very old-fashioned, too. I suppose you work so hard that you don't really have time to keep pace with modern thought. It is no longer a woman's crowning glory to be chaste. Love is no longer an emotion which has to last for ever. It comes and goes; it blows hot and cold. I have heard it called sex for fun, and you'd be surprised how many of my generation believe in it. Don't be afraid of it, Handsome, it's a wonderful thing.' Her voice had become husky, and she was smiling more widely. She moved one hand and stretched it towards him, as if she wanted to pull him down on top of her. 'You especially shouldn't be afraid,' she whispered. 'Have you forgotten how good looking you are? Have you forgotten that when you walk into a room every young girl looks up at you and starts to think about you, and to wonder what it would be like to have you alone, for an hour or for a night? You are an attractive male, a very attractive male, one of the most attractive males, and I don't think any one woman has an exclusive right to you.'

'Don't you?' he asked harshly.

'No,' she said. 'Roger, darling, stop pretending. Stop resisting.'

He would never be faced with greater temptation.

She seemed to sense that he was poised on the edge of indecision, that she had broken through his defences, and that soon she would be able to have her way. He moved back. She stretched out and took his hand, and said:

'Pull me up.'

He said, hard-voiced: 'You're wasting your time.' He pulled, and she pulled also, so that in a moment she was on her feet in front of him, only a foot or two away. She raised her hands, linked the fingers together and seemed about to place them on top of her head, but with slow, deliberate movements she lowered them behind her head, thrusting her bosom forward. He realized that she was unfastening the zipper of her dress. Even wearing that dress she was like a statue of a naked woman. She lowered her hands to her sides, then put her right hand up behind her, slowly, and moved it downwards; there was the faint sibilance of a zipper being pulled down.

Roger stood rooted there. Faith was still smiling, and he thought as he had thought in London that there was only one word for her: 'Desirable'. She was wholly desirable and beautiful, and his for the taking. She was woman and he was man, and they were together and there was no other place in the world.

He knew what she was going to do and he knew that he should stop her, that he should do something to break down the pose which seemed so natural to her.

She began to shrug her shoulders.

He reminded himself that he knew exactly what she was going to do; shrug that dress off her shoulders, shrug it until it fell and gathered about her waist, leaving her breasts bare or so nearly bare that it made no difference. And then she would slide the dress down over her long, lovely thighs and over her hips, and—

She murmured: 'Beautiful white skin, darling.'

The dress was off her shoulders. He was still staring at her. His mouth was parched. His skin felt dry on the forehead and on his cheeks. He kept wanting to moisten his lips, but did not. If he waited any longer it would be too late, and as he acknowledged that he found a question creeping into his mind, a question she had put there – a question which seemed to grow louder.

The question was: Why not?

The question became: She's utterly desirable, why shouldn't I take her?

And the question became: What's wrong about it?

The dress was right off her shoulders, now, tight for a moment across the tops of her breasts. She shrugged again and it began to fall lower, so that he could see the swelling shapes and the shallow valley between.

What was wrong about it? He needn't give her any information; she wouldn't be able to drag a word out of him, so – *why not?* Men did, thousands of men did, most men did. Didn't they? And it was not as if he would harm her, she was a self-confessed believer in free love, she would give herself wherever her fancy lay, with no thought of right or wrong. He felt quite sure that was true, he remembered something that Soames had said although he couldn't remember the words clearly, he couldn't remember anything clearly. He could only see Faith, *very* clearly. She seemed to be closer. Now the dress was gathered about her waist, and he saw that she had only a gossamer brassière on, holding her high and proud, concealing nothing.

It wouldn't do Janet any harm; she would never know; Janet would never know. Janet, Janet, Janet, Janet.

He was sweating.

There was a mist in front of his eyes and he did not understand it, but slowly it cleared, and then he could see that Faith had slipped the dress off and was stepping out of it. She wore no belt, nothing but the bra and close-fitting panties which hardly seemed to disturb the beautiful line of her figure.

She held her hands out towards him.

'Come, my darling,' she said.

He did not know why, but afterwards when he thought about it he believed that it was because she smiled as she spoke, and her smile seemed to say that she knew she had won, and that he could not resist her; her smile seemed to say that she was utterly sure of herself, and could destroy not only his resistance but also his will; could corrupt all that he believed in. Whatever the cause, a different kind of thought entered his mind, and a different mental picture. It was as if, when he had almost cried out: 'Janet, Janet, Janet, Janet,' he had been calling for her help, that he knew that without her he was lost; as if out of the depths of his sub-conscious there was a great need of her. He could see her. It seemed almost that she had come and answered his call, was standing behind Faith but could not draw nearer. She stood there and watched, but her expression seemed to say 'Choose me.' Whatever decision he made had to be his own, unaided.

The strange thing was that Janet was not the old Janet, young and lovely in her way, nor the Janet dressed for the occasion and looking at her striking best. It was the tired, rather careworn, rather remote Janet, and in the vision he could believe that she felt remote and aloof, that she knew there was nothing she could do except be with him.

'My darling,' Faith repeated softly. 'Take me.'

Words were like stones as Roger spoke.

'I'm going out,' he said. 'I'll be back in twenty minutes. If you're not gone when I return I shall telephone Wiess and tell him that I caught you here. That you'd forced entry. If you want to talk, I'll be downstairs in the foyer. We can eat together at the restaurant here.'

He saw the astonishment of utter disbelief in her eyes. They could never have been larger nor more beautiful. Nor had he seen her look so young, so like a child.

He turned away. He strode to the door. He fumbled for the latch, and it slipped from his fingers, so he made himself control them more firmly, and gripped the latch and opened the door. As he did so, a white-clad figure vanished, wraith-like, into another room along the passage, but he hardly noticed it. He closed the door, but it would not fasten, and suddenly, viciously, he tugged at it with all his strength, and it slammed with a crash of sound which seemed to shake the very walls and floor.

20

MORNING

HE WALKED down the stairs rather than be taken down by the diminutive lift-boy. Two parties of four were gathered in the hall, wearing evening-dress; they seemed to come from a different world. Two more swept in, and from a room out of sight there came the sound of music. Someone was singing a ballad. Roger looked about for the bar, found an *American Bar* sign and went into a box of a room with a coloured bar-tender and the usual miscellany of bright colours in the bottles behind the counter. He ordered a double Scotch, and tossed it down, ordered another, and sipped. The Indian bar-tender was watching him curiously. Two other men on their own sat at the bar, one of them with his face buried in his hands, his attitude strangely despondent. One or two couples were at tiny tables round the walls. Roger found the round-topped stool hard and uncomfortable. He felt low and almost depressed, without knowing why. He did not want to think. He finished the second drink and went into the foyer; more dancing couples were arriving, everyone seemed gay and carefree and happy.

The manager came up, also in dinner-jacket.

'Have you everything you require, Mr West?'

'Everything, thanks.' It had been a mistake to tell the girl that he would wait for her downstairs. But he hadn't. He said he would be back in twenty minutes, and if she wasn't out of his room he would call the police. It need not take her more than a few minutes to dress. Minutes? A few seconds, to pull that dress over that slim body. Would she have dinner with him? Had he been wise to suggest that they should eat together? The truth was that he did not want to make an enemy of her, but probably he had done that already. My God! What must she have felt like when he had turned away from her? Pride in her body, in her sex, in her ability to conquer a man, had all been spoiled. What would she do and how would she react?

He had been down for nearly half an hour, so he went upstairs by the lift. This time there was a tall, lanky boy on duty, lift attendants seemed to change very hour or so. He strode briskly along to his room, opened the door, and went in. He was not fully convinced that Faith would be gone; she might have decided to accept his challenge, and to try again.

She wasn't here.

There was a note on the stool on which she had sat, and he picked it up. It read: *I'll dine in my room.* Did that mean that she felt much the same as he, and didn't want to make an enemy of him? That kind of thing could cut both ways. He felt glad that she had taken the trouble to leave the note behind, and wondered whether he would be wise to telephone her. Not tonight, he decided, what kind of fool would that make of him? He went downstairs again, and out into the well-lit streets, and walked for twenty minutes until he came upon a restaurant with curtained windows, and the words *Cuisine Française* in gilt lettering across the glass panel of the door. He went in. The room was low-ceilinged, candle-lit, pleasant, and quiet, just right for his mood. A surprisingly youthful-looking man led him to a table in a corner where he was sheltered by a screen that appeared to be made of palm fronds. The menu seemed promising. There was background music, as at the hotel. He ordered a half-bottle of a South African claret and a *bifstek en casserole*, and found it delicious and satisfying. In one way it was a pity he was on his own, but in another it meant that he could let his thoughts drift over all aspects of the situation, and did not have to put up an act with other people. Before he had finished the meal he was thinking almost exclusively about the case, and even wondering whether he had been left on his own deliberately. That was an absurd thought. He began to think of Nightingale's story and the fact that Van der Lunn might be a serious suspect. What would Wiess and the Minister of Justice and all the rest think if that were the case?

By the time he was ready to leave, Roger felt almost normal, except that he was very tired, both physically and mentally; one good night's sleep would put that right. He went back to the hotel and upstairs, hoping that he would have no more shocks.

The suite was empty, but the bed had been turned down.

Last night he had slept in snatches on the aircraft, the night before he had been very late and wakeful, lying next to Janet. Janet, Janet, Janet, Janet. As he got ready for bed he wondered what she would think if she knew what had happened tonight.

He dropped off into deep, dreamless sleep – so absolute that although he heard the sound of a bell ringing he was not really conscious of what it was for a long time. There it rang, a million miles away, from another world but with an insistence which gradually brought awareness of it. *Brrr-brrr. Brrr-brrr.* Slowly, reluctantly, resentfully, he became aware of the urgency, became aware of the fact that it was to do with his waking life, not something he could ignore. So, slowly, he woke. The bell was the telephone bell, of course. It kept on and on. It was a long time before he was awake enough to know that he had only to stretch out his hand and lift the receiver to stop the ringing. There would be an obligation beyond that, one which he did not want.

He turned over, stretched out his hand and lifted the telephone. It was as smooth as a serpent, and slipped out of his grasp. It clattered on the floor, but at least the ringing stopped. Should he leave it there? He knew that he should not and knew that he wanted to above everything else. But he was awake now; his conscience as well as his consciousness were working together. He stretched down to the floor at the side of the bed and groped for the telephone. He heard a sound. He put the receiving end to his ear, and he heard a woman, shouting:

'Answer me – please answer me.'

A woman. In distress, in despair, in fear.

Her voice was shrill, touched with desperation.

'Please answer me!'

Roger said: 'Who's that? What do you want?' He was lying on his stomach, nearly halfway off the bed, but his mind was vividly alert; sleep was in the past and all he could think of was this woman.

'Handsome!' she cried, and her voice seemed to cut through him. 'I've been kidnapped. I'm in a village about halfway between Pretoria and Johannesburg.' He did not know whether the fear in her voice was real or pretended, whether this was another way to win his interest; he only knew that there seemed to be horror in her voice. Then she gasped: '*They're coming!*'

Roger said: 'Now listen. *Listen.* Where are you?'

'I'm on a road near Johannesburg, I tell you. A man – a man phoned and said he was a friend of Jim's. *I can see them* – two men. Handsome! I'm – scared.'

'What car is it?'

'A Ford, a Ford Consul.'

'Colour?'

'It's black. They're coming nearer – I can see them; they're slowing down.' He could hear the sound of a car engine. He thought he heard a man's voice, beyond Faith's. 'I'm on the outskirts of a village, there's a telephone – *they're coming.*'

'Are they black men or white?' He heard the bedroom door open and saw light streaming in from the passage and two men outlined against it: Percival and someone in police uniform. He called to them: 'Telephone Police Headquarters! There's been a kidnapping – the road between here and Johannesburg on the edge of a village.' He could hear the girl gasping for breath; it was easy to believe she was struggling. 'Handsome!'

And then she screamed.

And then the line went dead.

In the doorway, Percival was standing and staring. Along the passage a Bantu policeman was running very fast but making little sound. Roger banged the receiver back on to the platform, and rolled over and got up quickly. He sprang to his feet and ran towards the door; Percival dodged to one side as if he were scared. Roger reached the door of 501 and banged on it, but there was no answer.

'Open this door!' he roared at Percival.

The room-boy's hand was trembling so much that he could not insert the key. Roger snatched it away and thrust it in, turned the handle and flung the door open.

It was a large room, and the bathroom was on the right, a hanging cupboard with sliding doors on the left, and beyond these there was the foot of a double bed. There were some woman's clothes, neatly folded. He ran in, and saw the crumpled bedclothes and a pillow on the floor, a book on its face, a bedside lamp still alight, a pair of glasses by the book. So she had been to bed, and the call had come, and she had gone away in response to it.

.   .   .

Captain Standish was in the police-car with him. Another police-car was fifteen minutes ahead of them, and the Johannesburg police had been called out, too. Probably the whole of the police in the area had been alerted. Standish looked as wide-awake as if it were the middle of the morning, not the middle of the small hours; in fact, it was half past three. The sky was still vivid with stars. Very little moved, and there were no lights except in the distance, making a canopy over Johannesburg, and far behind them, over Pretoria.

Standish was saying: '... she must have gone through the kitchen, that was the only exit not watched. It looks as if she was kidnapped, but could she have been foxing?'

Roger said: 'Yes. I wondered if she was.' He did up the collar of his shirt, for it was cooler here by night than he had expected, and the heat generated by exertion and alarm had gone from him. He looked and felt dishevelled, but there was some satisfaction in the fact that it was less than half an hour since he had been called, and when so much had been put in hand.

He saw some red lights ahead; the rear lights of a car.

'What made you think she might have been lying to you?' Standish wanted to know.

'She tried to do a deal with me earlier in the evening. She

badly wanted to know what Nightingale had said. I turned her down. I had a feeling she might hate my guts because of that.'

'That kind of turn-down,' Standish said: there was a half sneer in his voice. 'Quite the soul of rectitude, aren't you?' Roger stared at the red light and saw some pale yellow lights on the right and left, and realized that they were approaching a village. Two cars were standing just off the road, and the headlights of another were coming from Johannesburg, the car swaying up and down. 'Looks as if they've found something. Did anyone else say anything?'

Roger said: 'She sounded as if she was hysterical with fear.' Then: 'No. I heard a car, and fancied there was a man's voice, that was all.' The driver slowed down, and a police-lieutenant came towards them. He put his head to the window close to Standish, and said:

'The Ford Consul was here, Captain.'

'Sure of that?' Standish pushed the door open.

'Yes, Captain. We have found a boy who was sneaking away from his girl-friend's quarters, and he saw the car. It was a dark one and a Consul – the boy works at a garage, he knows. He saw two men carry a struggling woman from the telephone box into the car.'

'We've an eye-witness!' Roger exclaimed as he scrambled out.

'For what it's worth,' said Standish.

At least this seemed to be confirmation of everything that Faith had said over the telephone.

Roger saw a little man standing between two Bantu police-men, some distance off the road, and saw two policemen searching the road and the telephone kiosk, one of them using a torch, the beam of which seemed very bright.

'It was too dark to see them properly, but he says they were white,' went on the lieutenant. 'We've sent a message back to Johannesburg, as it went in that direction,' he added. 'We'll get it.'

A man called out from the kiosk: 'Here's something.' He did not seem to realize who had arrived in the other car, but stood beckoning. Two more men moved towards the spot, one of them carrying an even larger torch. They converged on the kiosk and Roger was almost afraid of what they were going to find.

It was a tiny purse, wide-open. Some rand notes were folded and tucked into it, and there were pennies on the floor, and the glint of silver, too.

'And something else, Lieutenant,' said the man who had called out in that guttural voice. 'A torn dress, I think.'

'Dress,' echoed Roger.

Undoubtedly, it was part of a torn dress, the one which he had seen a few hours earlier as Faith had shrugged it off her shoulders. He was quite sure of the material and the colour as he fingered it and looked at it; and the shape and the edge showed that it had come off the neck.

'There isn't anything else we can do,' Standish said. 'But you can be sure we'll search for her as if she was worth all the missing diamonds. You'd better come back to Pretoria. I can imagine what you feel like, but this isn't a case for the Yard.'

.   .   .   .

It was half past four when Roger entered the bedroom again. He did not get undressed, but kicked his shoes off, undid his collar, and stretched out on the bed, quite sure that he would not get off to sleep again. His mind was working at top speed, sifting everything he knew and everything he suspected, separating facts from rumours and suspicions, trying to see what he knew existed in the pattern of events but was obscured or too complex. At least the kidnapping of the girl had jolted him out of the mood he had been in last evening; now he could look on her as someone in whom he had to be interested. There was no feeling of guilt in allowing himself to think about her.

He and Standish had asked the obvious question time and time again in the car coming back.

Why should anyone kidnap the girl?

There must be an answer.

As he lay there, feeling more sleepy than he had expected, Roger turned that question over and over in his mind, but could not get an answer. He had a feeling that it was so obvious that it was like something on the tip of his tongue, but it would not come.

Sleep did . . .

The second sleep was as deep as the first, but there was one big difference; when he woke, it was on the instant, without any sense of fear or of reluctance, and yet with a sense of urgency. The bell wasn't ringing. No one was tapping at the door. There was an unfamiliar sound, of rushing water – water running into a bath. Then he saw Percival, immaculate and smiling, step out of the bathroom.

'Baas take bath?' he inquired.

'Good idea,' Roger said. He glanced round. 'What time is it?'

'Half past seven, baas. This is going to be very busy day.' Percival's smile was enormous. 'You like yo' tea before bath or after it?'

'After. In ten minutes.'

'Yes, sah.' Percival went padding out. He had left a huge pink bath-towel hanging near the tub, and everything was in position, including a big loofah. Roger had a tepid bath followed by a cold shower, and was dabbing himself dry when Percival came in with the tea-tray. He put it down, appeared at the door and said: 'Tea ready, baas,' and went out. Roger stepped into the bedroom, mother-naked, pulled on his cotton pants, and then remembered that he had raised the blinds the night before. The offices of the bank directly opposite his window seemed to be peopled by girls all glancing this way. He pulled on a vest behind the bathroom door, and then went into the bedroom for the tea – and as he lifted the milk-jug, he saw a letter.

He picked it up, and read the printed words: *Cable & Wireless*. It was addressed to him care of Police Headquarters, so they hadn't lost much time sending it over. He poured out tea and then tore open the cable.

It read:

Joshua Bradshaw missing believed flying Johannesburg via Amsterdam stop. David Bradshaw had two banking accounts under assumed names totalling over fifteen thousand pounds Joshua one of eight thousand stop. First ten replies to police questionnaires in stop. Total commercial value of diamonds involved already over hundred thousand stop. Places involved so far Paris Brussels Amsterdam Madrid Stockholm Milan Dublin Lisbon London and Cairo stop. Signed Klemm.

Very softly, Roger began to whistle. He was still whistling, and thoughtful as well as anxious for news of Faith, when the telephone bell rang. He was nearly dressed, and feeling physically and mentally on top of himself; it was as if the conflict with Faith had cleansed both his mind and body. When he thought of that, he chuckled at the obvious implication.

'Roger West,' he said into the telephone. As he did so, he thought that this could be a message from or about Faith, that it might be of vital significance, and nothing at all seemed funny.

'This is Colonel Wiess's *aide*,' a man said in a deep, assured voice. 'Colonel Wiess's compliments, and he would like you to breakfast with him. He will be at your hotel at eight o'clock, and a room has been reserved.'

21

TACTICS

HE HASN'T slept all night, Roger thought as Wiess entered the room. The sun, slanting throught the venetian blinds, shone full on to his face and into his eyes, and he blinked and turned away quickly. The brick-red face was that of a man who spent a long time in the open air; there were one or two little red marks, suggesting that he had shaved in a hurry. As he shook hands with Roger, his eyes looked very tired and red-rimmed, but his grip hinted at his physical strength.

'I am sorry you had an anxious time last night,' he said. 'And I am also sorry that there is no news of Miss Soames. It is most regrettable, although there is reason to believe that it is partly her own fault.'

'Ah,' said Roger. 'Why?'

'It appears that she did receive the telephone call, the nature of which we do not know, and that she left the hotel by the kitchen exit, which was not under surveillance.' Wiess did not say whether he thought it should have been. 'A street patrol saw her driving out of the parking-place. The car was found near the telephone kiosk, abandoned.' Wiess stepped towards the window and adjusted the blind so that no direct light shone through. 'You permit that?'

'Of course.'

'I am sorry also to ask you to a conference so early in the morning,' Wiess went on, turning towards the table, which was beautifully laid, silver glistening, damask shining. 'However, I have urgent business during the day which I must attend. I am sure you understand.'

'Yes,' Roger said. 'Was the disturbance a bad one, Colonel?'

Wiess looked at him squarely. His eyes suddenly seemed less tired, as if the question had put him on the defensive, and wariness drove weariness away. Before he answered, there was a tap at the door. A European head-waiter with a French accent came in, followed by two Bantus in spotless white. The head-waiter presented the menu with a flourish; there were seven courses. Wiess hardly glanced at it, but said:

'Fish, steak, two eggs, sausages.'

'Very good, sir.'

'I'll have the same,' Roger decided.

'Would you like your steak well done, sir?'

'Medium well.'

'Like the Colonel always has his,' said the head-waiter; so breakfast-time sessions were not unusual. One of the Bantus came up with coffee, another poured out for Wiess and Roger; they were left to add their own hot milk. All of this Wiess took for granted, and he sipped the hot coffee until the waiters went out. The wariness had gone, and weariness was back.

'Yes,' he said, 'it was a bad night. Two Asians and three Bantus were killed before the police were able to quell the disturbance. It began over a dispute about seats on a bus. Why must there always be enmity and bloodshed?' He looked towards the window, and it was strange to see that strong and powerful face touched by an emotion which, if not grief, was certainly sadness. Then he squared his shoulders, and turned back to Roger. 'But this will not affect our inquiry, Superintendent. I have told you all about Miss Soames. It is now obvious that someone whom she knew or whom she believed she could trust telephoned her, and she went to see them. Something alarmed her, and she tried to escape from them. Her car tyre was punctured by a bullet. We have the bullet, a ·22 of Italian manufacture. That does not surprise you, does it?'

Bradshaw had been killed by a similar bullet.

'No,' Roger said heavily. 'It certainly doesn't. Have you any idea who the men were?'

'One was a small man, according to the witness.' Wiess gulped down another cup of coffee, and broke a roll and spread half of it liberally with butter. 'That does not surprise you, either. It has not been possible to get a detailed description, but what we do know tallies with your description of the man who murdered David Bradshaw. This, I understand, was probably one of two Italians, named Severini and Galli. Several men answering their descriptions have entered the country in the past forty-eight hours, some by air to the Jan Smuts Airport, some across the border with Southern Rhodesia, at Beit Bridge. These two men may be in the country. We cannot jump to conclusions, but neither can we ignore possibilities. You were about to say something?'

'Did you see the cable which reached me this morning?'

'I know nothing of it.'

'Bradshaw's brother has left England and the Yard thinks he's on his way here, *via* Amsterdam,' Roger said flatly.

Wiess made no comment, just stared. Roger took the cablegram from his pocket and handed it across the table.

Wiess took a long time reading it, and then said:

'You had no reason to suspect the brother, did you?'

'Not until now.'

'They do not say when he left, and it is possible that he will be here on the morning's KLM flight,' reasoned Wiess. 'It is not likely to arrive until midday or afterwards; there is good time to make sure this man does not enter the country.'

'I wonder if it's a good idea to hold him at the airport, or even to let him know that we've any idea who he is,' Roger suggested, very thoughtfully. Wiess made no comment, but waited to hear more. The door opened and the two Bantu boys came in, each bearing a silver salver. The hand which placed the fish on Roger's plate was as black as ebony. When they had retired, Roger went on: 'Did you have a chance to discuss Nightingale with the Minister of Justice?'

'Yes. I am to use my own discretion,' Wiess told him. 'Until the disappearance of Miss Soames I was inclined to agree with you that we should allow him to have freedom of movement in this country. Now—' He shrugged his powerful shoulders. 'You suggest that Joshua Bradshaw should have the same freedom, of course. It could be very dangerous. There are many ways out of this country, many borders which it is impossible to control thoroughly, places where those who know the country can slip across into Southern Rhodesia, even into Bechuanaland and South-West Africa.'

'If Nightingale and Bradshaw are going to take such a lot of trouble to get into the country, what makes you think they'll be so anxious to get out?'

'They will certainly be anxious to get out when they have achieved their objective, whatever it may be,' Wiess said drily.

It was impossible to argue against that.

'If we were looking for Nightingale, or simply watching him, we might lose him,' Roger conceded. 'If we watched Bradshaw as well, the chance of them both getting away would be pretty small.' He watched Wiess fork the white fish, and ate a little himself; it wasn't particularly tasty, but went down easily enough. He finished, forced a smile, and went on: 'I know, it's easy for me to suggest the best course of action; I'm not familiar with the kind of problems you know you'll run up against.' Wiess still did not comment, but finished his fish and pushed his plate back. 'There's one fairly obvious thing I didn't see until you were telling me what happened to Faith Soames.'

'What is that?'

'If Nightingale is telling the truth, he was framed so that you would prevent his moving freely about the country. Now an associate from *The Globe* is lured out of her room and then kidnapped. The same people could be involved for the same motive.'

'What motive?' demanded Wiess.

Roger shrugged. 'That's one of the answers we're looking for. One possibility is that they want to find out what she knows – and they wanted to find out what Van der Lunn knew.'

There was another tap on the door and the two waiters came in, this time with enormous silver dishes laden with more food. Roger watched as the black hand placed a large steak with two large sausages, some strips of bacon, two eggs, and some tomatoes on his plate, then placed the tray by his side; there was at least as much left on it.

'We'll help ourselves,' Wiess said, and the boys went off, long white gowns rustling slightly. Wiess ate solidly for several minutes, paused, and asked:

'So you would release Nightingale, allow Joshua Bradshaw to enter freely, and follow both in the hope that they would lead you to Faith Soames.'

'And the rest of the answers,' Roger said.

'Ah. Yes. It would need a large force of men, there would have to be no chance of either of them disappearing. Ach.' Wiess reminded Roger a little of Hardy in that moment; it was the first time he had thought of Hardy since he had arrived in South Africa. He did not try to persuade the Colonel, who was no more likely than Hardy to be persuaded about anything against his better judgement.

Suddenly, Wiess said: 'We will try it. Both men must be here for a purpose. Yes, we will try it.' He looked pleased that he had made the decision, and tucked into the rest of the food, helped himself to another steak, and ate that with as much relish as he had the first; Roger gave up after a fourth sausage. The Bantus came in with fresh coffee, and Wiess watched them pour out, then waved them away. 'You understand, of course, that you will not be able to take any part in following them, for you would be recognized at a glance. We shall keep you fully informed. Captain Standish will be in charge here. We shall use Bantu detectives, for we find that people from England take Bantus for granted in our country. They do not suspect they are detectives!' Wiess gave the faintest of smiles. 'I wish I could take personal charge, but it is not possible today or tomorrow. And in that time it is possible that there will be some results.'

'I hope so,' Roger said. 'One thing.'

'What is it?'

'If the time comes when I can do anything, will you make sure I get the chance?'

This time, Wiess smiled quite broadly.

'Yes,' he said. 'I shall weigh up the balance between allowing a senior officer from Scotland Yard to be in danger, and of losing the services of a very capable man. Remember, we are as anxious as you to find the answer to our questions.' The smile faded. 'In some ways we are more anxious. We have had a message from Scotland Yard this morning, about Mr Van der Lunn. He is neither better nor worse, and is still on the danger list. The consequences could be very serious if he were to die, especially if this mystery is unsolved.' He paused, broodingly, and then went on: 'To start with, you may wish to see Nightingale again and to tell him that he will not be detained, although we shall hold his passport until we have satisfied ourselves that he has told the truth.

'I'd want to tell him that the girl is missing, too, and what happened to her,' Roger said.

'That is permissible.' Wiess stood up, tall and very erect. 'We shall need a little time to make sure that the arrangements for watching Nightingale are completed. It will also be advisable for you to be at the airport when the KLM plane arrives, so that you can identify Joshua Bradshaw. You see, we shall not allow you to laze your time away.'

22

LIE?

Nightingale looked much more rested and untroubled than Wiess had. A newspaper was open at the foot of his bed, which was made; he had shaved, and there was impatience in his manner as Roger appeared by the cell bars, but he restrained this impatience until the door had opened, Roger was inside, and the door was closed and locked again.

'One way of telling me you didn't do a good job,' Nightingale said harshly. 'I wonder if you really tried. I wrote that statement exactly as I told the story to you, and—'

Roger interrupted: 'How well do you know Faith Soames?'

Nightingale took a moment or two to adjust himself to the change of subject, and then asked sharply:

'What's she got to do with it?'

'Just answer my question.'

'She's got as keen a mind as her uncle, she doesn't know how to say no or how to allow anyone else to say no, and she has a memory like an electronic computer. Does that answer your question?'

'Yes. Did she know what you were coming here for?'

'No. West, what's all this about?'

Roger said: 'She decided she ought to come and hold your hand. She came, she tried to be clever, and she got herself kidnapped. No one knows where she is. Do you know where she might be?'

Nightingale breathed: 'My God.'

He backed to the bed, and sat down.

'My God,' he repeated. 'Faith.'

Roger asked sharply: 'Do you know who might have kidnapped her and where they might have taken her?'

Nightingale gulped. 'I—' he began, and then his eyes narrowed, and it seemed to Roger that something jelled in his mind; the shock was over, and he was beginning to think again, was probably beginning to lie. 'No,' he said, and then in a louder voice: 'Why the hell should I know who would do a thing like that?'

'You came here to look for someone – who was it?'

Nightingale said: 'I came here to see if I could pick up any more information about Van der Lunn. This was one time when he couldn't stop me. That's all.' His mouth seemed like a trap as he went on: 'What are the bloody cops doing to find her?'

'Scouring the countryside.'

'If anything happens to her—'

'If anything happens to her it will be her own fault, just as it will be your own fault if anything happens to you.'

'Nothing can happen to me in this bloody place.' Nightingale moistened his lips. 'My God, what will old Soames say? He worships her. Why the hell did he let her come? Why – West!' Nightingale gripped Roger's shoulder. 'Does he know she's missing?'

'Not yet.'

'He's got to be told. Do you hear? He's got to be told – and I've got to get out of this place.' His voice grew louder. 'If you've any influence at all, get me out of here so that I can talk to Soames, and so that I—' He broke off, gritting his teeth. 'It's like being in a cage. I can't take it. Understand – I can't take it.'

'You'll have to take a lot worse for a lot longer if you play the fool again,' Roger said. 'They're holding your real passport so that you can't leave the country until they've checked on your story – and if you leave illegally you'll never be able to come back. Is that clear?'

Nightingale said wonderingly: 'You mean they'll let me go?'

'Yes.'

Nightingale frowned. 'Well, that's something. That's certainly something.' After a pause he asked sharply: 'Am I restricted to Pretoria?'

'No.'

Nightingale gave a fierce grin, and slapped Roger on the shoulder. The power in his arm was very great, the slap was almost painful.

'So you did your stuff. I won't forget it.' New life seemed to be pouring into him even as he stood there, and suddenly he clapped his hands together with a resonant bang. 'Will I be glad to move about again! This has been hell.' He broke off. 'When are they going to let me out?'

'Now.'

'How soon can I get through to Soames?' demanded Nightingale.

. . .

Standish, back on duty, put a small office with two telephones at Roger's disposal. It was a little after nine o'clock in Pretoria, six o'clock in London. Nightingale had given Soames's home number, and complained bitterly when he was told there would be an hour's delay.

'Except for priority, calls sometimes take a day,' Standish had said. 'Think yourself lucky.'

Nightingale was trying to bury his impatience in the *Johannesburg Star*. Roger was sifting through reports from Pretoria and Johannesburg about the hunt for Faith and her kidnappers. Whenever he thought of the girl, he had a tense feeling of anxiety, quite sure that when she had called him she had been in terror; and probably for the first time in her life she had come up against this kind of harsh reality. There were photographs of her from the newspaper files. There were also photographs of her car, the nearside rear tyre worn to ribbons where she had driven on it in desperation; and of the bullet, a *Lambetti* ·22. There were photographs of the rifling on the bullet, of the tyre-tread of the Ford Consul as well as Faith's Jaguar, and there were fingerprints, blown up to twenty times their normal size. These were Faith's and those of a dozen other people who had been in the telephone kiosk fairly recently. Roger had the same sense of organization and thoroughness and of everything being under complete control as he had at the Yard.

The strangeness of the fact that everyone here was in uniform was wearing off; they might look and sometimes behave like soldiers, but they were just as much policemen as the CID at home.

'When the hell's that call coming through?' Nightingale muttered. He flung the newspaper aside. 'Can't you do anything to hurry it?'

Roger didn't answer, but passed him some of the reports and then read a time-table of reports about black or dark blue or dark green Ford Consuls which had been seen in the vicinity during the night or in the early hours of the morning. Four were marked with a red asterisk; these were cars whose owners had not been traced. One of them, registration number SX2134, had been singled out for special attention, because of its speed, just as one might have been in Greater London. It had been seen racing through the suburbs of Johannesburg away from Pretoria, travelling through the towns of Heidleburg and Rensdorp, and was known to have joined the National Road from Johannesburg to Durban about forty miles out of Johannesburg. Wiess had put out a general call for it, and all its movements would now be traced.

A telephone bell rang. Nightingale jumped up and snatched at the receiver, grated: 'Hallo?' then muttered under his breath and thrust the instrument into Roger's hand. 'For you.'

'West,' said Roger, quietly.

'Have you seen the reports on the Consuls?' It was Standish, from next door.

'I've just finished,' Roger replied.

'We've had two more on SX2134,' Standish said. 'It's still heading towards Durban. It's being driven by a small man who might possibly answer the description we had last night, and a bigger man is sitting next to him. There's no report of a passenger, but three reports say that rugs are spread over the back.'

'Is it being followed?' Roger asked.

'Yes, by a patrol car of the Orange Free State. It will be picked up by Natal police very soon.'

'And stopped and searched?'

'Yes, of course.'

Nightingale was leaning across Roger's desk when he rang off, and their faces were very close together. Roger wondered about the man's relationship with Faith, whether he had a much deeper personal reason for anxiety than he had yet said.

'Was that about Faith?'

'Might be, might be not,' said Roger. 'The police are not missing any tricks, and—'

The telephone bell rang again, and once more Nightingale snatched up the receiver, only to hand it to Roger, for it was the call to London. He stood up very straight, staring at the wall over Roger's head, in much the way that Soames had in his office. Roger motioned to the extension telephone. There were noises on the line, words like: 'You there, London?' and 'This is London, one moment, please,' and then suddenly Soames's voice sounded; and there was no doubt that it was *The Globe* editor; his voice had a timbre which could not be mistaken even over six thousand miles.

'Hallo. Is that you, Faith?'

Nightingale said: 'No, Jack, it's not.'

'*Jim!*' Soames's voice changed its tone. 'Don't tell me she managed to get you out, you half-wit. How are you?'

'I'm fine. Jack, I've got bad news for you. Faith didn't get me out; West did that.'

'Who?'

'Handsome *West.*'

'Oh, the copper. Good for him. How's Faith?'

'Jack,' Nightingale said, 'Faith's been sticking her neck out, and—'

Soames chuckled.

'I'll bet she has. Have you ever known her keep it in? How is she?'

Nightingale was finding it difficult to put the truth into words. Now, although he should have given the answer, he moistened his lips and gulped. Again it occurred to Roger that he might feel deeply for the girl.

'Are you there?' Soames demanded.

'Mr Soames, this is Roger West,' Roger said. 'I'm sorry to tell you that your niece is missing, sir. We have every reason to believe that she has been taken away against her will.' He gave Soames a chance to comment, but when the old man did not take it, he went on: 'The South African police are doing everything they can to find her, and you can be sure that once she is found we'll look after her.'

Soames said: 'Missing? Kidnapped?'

'Yes.'

'Who—' Soames seemed to choke. 'West!'

'Yes, sir?'

'You've got to find her.'

'Everything possible is being done,' Roger said. 'There's one thing you can do.'

'What is it?'

'Tell Nightingale that if he knows anything or even suspects anything about this, if he can even guess where Faith might be, he must tell the police.'

After a pause, Soames said: 'Yes. My God, yes. Jim – are you there?'

'I heard,' said Nightingale, stiffly.

'Tell them everything you can. D'you hear me? Tell them everything. You're always holding out on me, you're always telling me you know what's best, but don't hold out on the police over this. Not over Faith. She – *West*?'

'Yes, sir?'

'Do you think she is in danger?'

'She could be,' Roger said.

'Jim,' said Soames, thickly, 'you heard West, you heard me. If you know anything, tell the police. Hear me? Tell them.'

.   .   .

'If I knew anything at all I would tell you,' Nightingale said. 'But I don't know a thing.'

Roger felt almost sure that he was lying.

.   .   .

Standish asked a few routine and formal questions: where

Nightingale intended to go, where he proposed to stay, whether he intended to travel by air, road, or rail. Nightingale was obviously champing at the bit, and when at last he stalked off, saying that he was going to Johannesburg to consult his newspaper's office there, Roger felt that he was carrying a tremendous burden. Standish stood at the window and looked out, and Roger joined him and saw the newspaperman striding purposefully along the street. The only other people on foot in the street were Bantus.

'We'll know, wherever he goes,' Standish said confidently. 'Any idea what he's keeping back?'

'No. I've an idea why he might want to keep something back, though. He may think he can do a private deal for the release of the girl. Supposing he tries? What will you do?'

'Supposing we wait for it to happen,' said Standish almost sharply. He waited until Nightingale turned out of the street, and as he went back to his desk his telephone bell rang. He picked up the instrument as if he had all the time in the world. 'Captain Standish.' It was a considered pose, of course. He was out to impress Roger all the time. Suddenly his expression changed and all pretence was dropped. 'The fools!' he roared. 'Where ... Yes ... Damaged? ... On *fire*.'

Roger stood rigidly by the desk. Judging from Standish's manner, this was shocking news. He saw a mind picture of Faith Soames, as she had been in his room last night, leaning back and tempting him, quite sure that he could not resist her.

'Use aircraft, of course,' said Standish. '*Of course*.' He banged down the receiver and stared at Roger, and for the first time Roger saw him really shaken. 'That Consul went over a cliff in the foothills of the Drakenberg, near Ladysmith. It caught fire. The police in the car which picked up its trail lost it on a by-road. The driver was obviously trying to evade them. It isn't yet known whether the occupants were injured or not. It isn't even certain whether they were in the car when it went over the edge.' Standish was clenching his hands tightly, and Roger wondered if, in fact, there was worse to come, when he went on: 'The accident occurred only thirty miles from Van der Lunn's mountain home.'

23

TOWARDS THE MOUNTAINS

ROGER COULD picture old Soames's despair, knowing how much the girl meant to him. He could picture the blazing wreckage of the car at the foot of a ravine, and he could almost see the way the flames devoured the human flesh and blood. But there was no certainty that it had happened. He wanted to go to the scene and be on the spot when the rescue party went down to see if there was anything left to rescue, but he knew that was impossible.

Standish was saying:

'. . . it's time we got there.'

'Where?'

'The airport,' Standish said.

Roger stared; and then he remembered Joshua Bradshaw.

'How long will it take us to get there?'

'Half an hour,' Standish said. 'I wish—' He broke off when his telephone bell rang again, and snatched it up, quite as anxious as Nightingale had been. 'Captain Standish? . . . Very good.' His tension left him, but exasperation replaced it as he put the receiver down. 'I have a verbal report to make,' he said. 'I cannot come personally to the airport. I will send Lieutenant Lukas with you, and he'll do everything he can to help. All you have to do is make sure the man is on the aircraft, and if he is, point him out.'

'There's someone else I could probably identify,' Roger said.

'Who?'

'Faith Soames.'

Standish looked as if that comment took him by surprise. He frowned, then shrugged it off without comment, just 'I daresay.' He pressed a bell, and a very tall Lieutenant of Police came in. He had thick hair at the back of his head, but was almost bald in front – and again that reminded Roger of a Bradshaw; of Rebecca, with her hair straight back from her forehead and then a frizzy mop behind the band which held it in place. He had met Lukas already, and obviously the policeman had been briefed.

'The important thing is to keep out of this man's sight,' said Standish.

'Yes. If you have any word of the girl, can you let me know?'

'I will telephone a message to the airport,' Standish promised. His telephone rang again. He answered it quickly, then shook his head at Roger, and gave full attention to the call. Lukas led the way out of the office, out of the building, into a police-car with a Bantu driver waiting to take the wheel. Traffic was thick, and for the first time Roger realized that driving habits here were different from London, and the drivers seemed to take even more chances. One man cut in almost savagely as they approached a junction; another car cut in from the other side. Roger's heart was in his mouth, but the police-driver seemed to accept it as normal.

He drove fast once they were on the open road, heading for the airfield at Kempton Park. The roads were good and straight, there were a lot of young pine trees lining some of them, and some new housing estates. Outside the airport there was a huddle of taxis and private cars, and an air of eager anticipation. As they drove through the main gates, the driver spoke to a guard in Bantu, and then reported in English:

'It is due in five minutes, sir.'

'Just good time,' Lukas remarked.

Roger half expected some word from Standish, but there was no message, and he told himself that it was folly to expect one. Why should he be so edgy about that girl? Would he have been, had it been anyone else? He didn't know. Soon they were led by an airport police-lieutenant to the control-tower, and to a seat close to a man wearing earphones and talking into a mouthpiece; obviously he was giving landing instructions. On a radar screen on one side there was the light dot which showed the aircraft coming in to land. An atmosphere of bustle was everywhere. Bare-legged and bare-footed porters, mostly tall and handsome and very fit, pushed barrows and trucks towards the spot where the airliner would come in. Two ambulances and two fire-engines stood ready for emergency, a fuelling truck was in position.

What had seemed at first a dot in the sky soon became a recognizable shape, but there was little noise in the control-tower. The radio was silent now. The aircraft appeared to be straight in front of them, losing height rapidly. Yet it still seemed a long way off. It touched down, seemed to bound, touched again, and then with a lordly air of disdain, it slowed down on the runway and came gently to a stop.

Soon, the steps were pushed into position, the door of it opened, a stewardess appeared, then two officers, then the passengers began to straggle out.

The fifth man was quite unmistakably Joshua Bradshaw.

.   .   .

Bradshaw had a passport in the name of Bell, but every-thing else on it seemed to be accurate. Roger wondered how often he used it, and how long he had had it; they were questions which must soon be answered, but he had no time to worry about them then.

Lukas, by Roger's side, was already on the telephone to Standish. Roger watched the man whom he had last seen at Common View Hotel as he walked towards the Customs offices. It was very hot out there, and Joshua seemed to be sweating; he kept dabbing at his forehead with a grubby handkerchief. He kept looking round, too, almost as if he were fearful, and seemed to enter the Customs offices with relief.

Lukas said: 'Yes. He is here.' He handed the telephone to Roger. 'The Captain would like to talk to you.'

Roger said: 'Hallo?' And his heart began to thump.

'I can tell you one more thing,' said Standish. 'Nightin-gale went to the Johannesburg newspaper offices as he said, but left after five minutes. He has borrowed one of the newspaper's cars, and is now heading south-east, along the main Johannesburg–Durban road towards the Drakenberg. It is beginning to look as if he and the others will converge there.'

'We'll soon know where Bradshaw's going, as well,' Roger said.

'If he heads for the same direction, then I think you should, too,' said Standish. 'Stay there until we've some news – I've given Lukas instructions. If Bradshaw hires a car or is met by one, and heads for the Drakenberg, then I think we ought to fly to Ladysmith. That is near the place where the car went over, and by the time we reach there we shall know whether that car had passengers or not. Are you ready to fly?'

'Any time,' Roger said.

'I thought you would be,' Standish said drily. Something seemed to have put him in a much better mood. 'I'll come back as soon as I can.'

He rang off. Roger moved to the other side of the control-tower, and was then taken out along the roof until he could see the passengers as they cleared Customs and went to the waiting taxis and cars. Bradshaw went to a big black Chrysler, and a man in a chauffeur's uniform came up and saluted by touching the peak of his cap. They shook hands. There seemed to be no formalities at all, but Bradshaw got in, and took the wheel. It was a moment or two before Roger realized the significance of that.

Lukas said: 'It is a private-hire car, of the drive-yourself kind. I think that Bradshaw will drop the chauffeur at some convenient point, and then drive on by himself.'

Roger watched as the Chrysler moved off, turned two corners, and shot out of the main gates. It swung towards Johannesburg.

'He knows the airport and knows the road,' Roger said. 'He's probably been here often before.'

'I think you are certainly right,' said Lukas.

.   .   .

Two smaller aircraft came in during the next half an hour,

while Roger made a pretence of looking over the airport buildings. The sun was very hot, but the air so dry that he did not feel it except on the back of his head; he wished he had a hat with him. There was no shop near by. He ought to buy something to cover his head. If he were going to be out in the sun often he would need one. He kept passing his hands over the back of his head. Lukas took him to the airport restaurant for a drink or coffee; he chose coffee. He had nearly finished when a Bantu policeman in immaculate uniform came up and saluted.

'You are required on the telephone, Lieutenant. There is one close by.' He led the way to a telephone in the wall, took off the receiver and handed it to Lukas. No one else appeared to take any notice of them at all.

Lukas said: 'Yes ... Yes, Captain ... He *has*?' There seemed a very long pause before he spoke again, and then it was with obvious satisfaction. 'Very good, sir. I will.' He put the receiver down, turned to Roger, and said: 'Bradshaw dropped the chauffeur outside the hire company's garage in Eloff Street, and then went off along the National Road towards Durban. Nightingale has already driven sixty miles along the same road.'

'Sixty?'

'You are not used to our fast main roads,' Lukas told him. 'Are you ready?'

'When you are.'

'The aircraft is waiting,' announced Lukas. 'It is an old converted Dakota, larger than we require, but the only one available. The pilot and co-pilot have been given their instructions, and the engines are already warming up.'

Roger said: 'That's fine.' He stepped out of the shade of the building, and the sun struck very hot on his head again as he walked with Lukas to the aircraft, which was farther away than the jet airliner. That was already being refuelled and made ready for its homeward flight. By the time they reached the old-fashioned-looking Dakota, Roger was sheltering the back of his head with his hand, but once they were in the shade of the aircraft's cabin, he forgot the heat. He felt the aircraft quivering as he stepped inside, and saw that there were only ten seats; the rest of the space had been cleared for freight. The pilot was an unexpectedly plump and elderly man, probably in his sixties, the co-pilot looked hardly old enough to have his licence, but they did everything with a brisk efficiency and the take-off could not have been smoother.

'Visibility and conditions perfect,' the co-pilot announced. 'Ever flown here before, Superintendent?'

'Never been to Africa before.'

'I can't speak for all of it, but South Africa's a beautiful country,' the youngster said. He reminded Roger of Richard, clean-cut and nice looking, with bright eyes and rather curly, dark hair, but above all he had something of Richard's enthusiasm. 'One of the most beautiful on earth.' Roger wondered if he had seen many other countries: could he be more than twenty-one or two? 'Like me to point a few things out, sir?' He pointed them out regardless. 'You can see Pretoria from here. Ought to see it at jacaranda time, it's magnificent. Magnificent. I've never seen anything like it. See the Union Buildings? ... The Voortrekker Monument? ... Now over there you can really see what Johannesburg looks like from the air. Bit of a laugh to say that it's like New York – they say that about Sydney, too – but all the same those tall buildings are pretty impressive. The zoo and the park are a damned sight safer than Central Park in New York by night, even though Jo'burg's supposed to be such a deadly place ... That's the new Johannesburg Hotel – they certainly needed a new one. American money, you can bet ... See the slag heaps over there, and the mine workings? They say the Rand is nearly played out, but you ought to see the new mines down at Welkom, fantastic place, as new in planning as anything they have in the United States. I must say that for them.'

The slag heaps and the city were already falling behind them. The river Vaal looked dark, almost black, with the mud which rains had washed along a thousand tiny tributaries. The sky was a metallic blue, and the sun looked like a ball of fire, but it was pleasantly cool in the cabin.

'Do you know the United States well?' asked Roger.

'It depends what you call well,' said the co-pilot, with a broad grin. 'I've worked for three of the major airlines over there, had a few years with Cunard Airlines in little old England first. Absolutely love flying. Love it. Best way to see the world, too, but I've got a feeling that when I've got tired of travelling I'll come back here. Here, or the West Coast of America – they're the two places for my money. Now you won't see very much for a while, but before long you'll see the Drakenbergs rising up into the sky – fantastic sight when you approach them from a reasonable height. We'll go in at about three thousand. Have to fly down in the valleys if you're going into any of the mountain cities. Why don't I show you some maps and pictures, and leave you alone for a bit?'

The pilot called: 'Good idea, you son of a cackler.'

Roger found himself smiling. He relaxed as he looked through the coloured illustrations of the Drakenberg Mountains and of Basutoland.

'Boy, is that rugged country up in Basutoland. Take it from me it's wild and woolly ... I went up there once, and nearly got lost. If it hadn't been for a little Basuto belle I probably would have been! She'd got lost, too, and all her family were out looking for her. Grandma to grandpa down to baby sister. Dozens of them. Nearly got myself in trouble that time, because she was as naked as the day and I was pretty hot and stripped down to jockey shorts. Or do you call them Y-pants? ... I want Tubby up there to start a new tourist service, kind of airborne safari; the only way to get to some of these inaccessible places. You could "do" Africa damned well in four weeks, and with a crate like this we could carry plenty of freight, too. Make a fortune.'

'Make a fool of yourself,' called out the pilot. 'Hey, Lieutenant, we were asked to look out for a fire.'

Roger felt tension coming back.

'Yes,' called Lukas.

'How would that do?' The pilot pointed to his right, towards the south, and they moved towards the windows and looked out. A faint haze of grey smoke was coming from the rocky country below, not far from the ribbon-like twisting road. 'Looks like a car gone over the edge to me,' the pilot continued. 'Wouldn't be much chance for the poor devils if that happened.'

Roger, peering intently, thought he saw the movement of men. As the aircraft turned in a half circle, and veered over steeply, they could see the other side of the ravine, the sun glinting on three cars, and men on the rocky slopes between the road and the ravine.

'Looks to me as if they're coming up,' the pilot said. 'Would you like to borrow my glasses?'

They were a huge pair of field-glasses, which looked as if they were antiques from the First World War, but as Roger focused them, he saw the tangled wreckage of the car clear through a thin haze of blue-grey smoke. There was a kind of track leading away from this and he raised the glasses until he could see the men. There were eight of them altogether, and they seemed to be climbing upwards, away from the wreckage.

Nearer the mountains and towards the Indian Ocean was a tiny white speck, and very near it a big slag heap, pale grey in colour, and the wheel of a mine.

'Van der Lunn's home and Van der Lunn's diamond mine,' the pilot said. 'One of the oldest families in South Africa, the Van der Lunns. He's the last. His wife died years ago and he's got no children. But he always comes back there – got luxury flats in Johannesburg and Sea Point in the Cape, travels round the world – but this is home. Hardly has time to take any personal interest in the mine these days – it's run by a manager. Well – we'd better get down.'

Fifteen minutes later they landed at the Ladysmith airfield, little more than a landing strip. Half a dozen brightly-coloured private aircraft were clustered near the small office building, as well as a helicopter and several cars, two of them with a police sign up.

Two policemen, one a white lieutenant, one a Bantu sergeant, came smartly towards them. Roger forced himself to wait until Lukas asked:

'Have you a report on that burned-out car?'

'Yes, we have,' said the lieutenant promptly. 'There was no one in it. It was pushed over the edge. The passengers must have gone off in another car, and we don't know what it was like. We're making inquiries.'

24

VAN DER LUNN'S HOUSE

So FAITH SOAMES hadn't perished in that fire, Roger thought with deep relief.

He felt the heat of the sun strike at him again as he studied the lieutenant who had brought the news, a rock-like-looking individual who might almost have been carved out of the stone of the great range of mountains. There they were in the distance, towering into the sky, massive and forbidding despite the fierce sunlight.

The pilot and co-pilot were unloading wooden boxes of freight. Roger, Lukas, and the lieutenant walked towards the shade of some small trees, and Lukas asked:

'Is there any news of Nightingale?'

'No,' the lieutenant answered. 'We've a lookout post up near the fork in the road, and two-way radio contact. We would have heard if there was any word.'

'He wouldn't have had time to get here,' Roger said.

'He could have, if he travelled fast enough,' said Lukas. 'How soon can we be at the lookout post, Lieutenant?'

'In an hour,' the local man answered. 'Will you start right away?'

'We can't start too soon for Superintendent West,' said Lukas earnestly. They moved off towards one of the police-cars. This time the lieutenant took the wheel and they did not have a Bantu with them. Roger sat in front with him, Lukas in the back. It was no more eventful to them than it would have been to Roger had he stepped into a Divisional car in a London suburb, but here he felt the strangeness of Africa, a sense of being somewhere remote and close to the primeval. As the car turned out of the airfield, two native women, arms and ankles covered in beads, great necklaces of tiny beads draped round their necks, walked along the dusty road without taking any notice of the car. Their smooth brown skin seemed to shimmer in the sunlight, the fine full breasts seemed to sway in a solemn dance as they walked along. Not far away, they turned off the main road on to a narrow dirt one which led towards the mountains, and in the distance Roger saw the round native huts, the kraal, from some of which he could see smoke rising. A big truck with a skinny Bantu driver and a dozen Bantus standing in the back came tearing past, ignoring them, but covering them with a great cloud of dust. The two policemen seemed to take it for granted.

The road became steeper. There were rocky slopes on either side, and they seemed to be climbing all the time. Now and again the powerful engine of the car appeared to stutter in protest, but it always picked up. Soon, they were buried in the foothills of the mountains. Here and there they passed the mouth of a small mine, long since deserted, but apart from that there was rock and scrub and little else, until they came to a sign which read: *Main Road* in both English and in Afrikaans. They crawled up a sharp rise on to the main road, and immediately swung off it again up a narrow trail which seemed impossibly steep. The engine seemed to groan, but at last the terrain flattened out, and Roger realized that they had drawn in behind a huge rock which seemed to be of solid granite. A police-car was standing in the shadow, close to the rock, hidden from the road. A small tent was near the car, there was a wooden picnic-table, some tins of food and an ice-box, as there might be for any party camping out. On one side there were magnificent views of the mountains, rising in spiked pinnacles into the sky; behind them was the massive rock with some natural holes, like caves, created over the centuries by the erosion of wind and rain and cold.

A European police-sergeant was climbing down from one

of these holes. Behind him, still in the hole, were two Bantus, another European sergeant and a European constable, who took no notice of the newcomers.

'I am very glad to meet you, sir,' the first sergeant said as he shook hands with Roger. 'And very proud if I can be of help. No car has passed since we came, but I am informed that a car with two Europeans and one European woman passed on the way to Mr Van der Lunn's house earlier this morning.'

'Now we know what happened,' Lukas said confidently. 'This car was waiting for them when they reached a certain spot. They pushed the Ford over, and finished the journey in a Volkswagen. Looks to me as if someone left it off the road for them. There's one good thing: the woman is alive.' He turned to Roger. 'Would you like to see where we watch the road from?'

'Very much.'

'Just follow me,' said the sergeant, and as they moved up to one of the spy-holes, he went on: 'Will you speak with Sergeant Hombi? He is most excited at the prospect of working with you; he knows of your fame in England.'

'Of course,' Roger said.

Hombi was lying flat on his stomach and watching the distant road through binoculars. There was room for all of them to lie side by side, and the constable took the glasses as the sergeant said:

'Hombi, this is Superintendent West.'

Hombi might almost have been Jameson's twin brother, Roger thought; he had the same good looks, the same kind of reserved and almost diffident smile, and at the same time a self-confidence which gave a good impression.

'Would you like to look through the glasses, sir?'

'Very much,' said Roger.

Hombi tapped the constable on the shoulder, took the glasses, then stretched out on his stomach again, with Roger beside him. The far end of the cave seemed to make a kind of telescope in itself; in the distance they could see the road winding through the mountains, a tiny ribbon crossing savage stretches of rock and winding round jagged slopes in a series of hairpin bends. With the glasses, everything was so much nearer; it was like looking out on to a mountain wilderness.

'You see any movement, sir?'

'No,' Roger said. He held the glasses to his eyes for another minute, hopefully, then wriggled out of position and handed them over. As he stood up near Lukas and the other European officers, it seemed much warmer, even in the shade of the rock, than in the hole itself. The sun was moving round slowly, and there was a bright stretch of sunlight only a yard or two away; heat seemed to creep from it. But it was not the brightness of the sun nor the desolation of the scene which worried him. He could not repress his anxiety any longer; his problem was to explain it in words which would cause no offence.

'Lieutenant,' he said to Lukas, 'what will happen if Nightingale and Bradshaw pass along here?'

'We shall move in,' Lukas answered, simply.

'But won't they be a long way ahead of us?'

Lukas frowned. 'I do not understand you.' It was easy to imagine from his expression that he had sensed criticism, and was ready to react against it. 'If they are not at the house or the mine, how can we move against them? It was you yourself who said that until we know where they are going and what they are planning to do, there is nothing we can do.'

Roger said gruffly: 'Yes, I did. But there's only the one road to Van der Lunn's house and the mine. They could block it.'

To his surprise and great relief, Lukas grinned broadly; he was really little more than a boy. The two other Europeans were equally amused, the block of a man turning a laugh into a snort. Roger waited.

'Let me show you,' Lukas said. He took another set of binoculars from the table near the tent, and put a hand on Roger's shoulder, then led him farther along the rock table. The sun struck fiercely at Roger's head, but soon they were in shade again; sunlight, shade, heat, and coolness, and all the time uncertainty about Lukas and the others. They reached a ledge a hundred yards away from the camp. The remarkable thing was that the whole panorama changed; now they were looking in the other direction, at the sun-bleached rocks and scrub, and the distant house seemed as if it were made of marble, it was so white. Less than a mile away, Roger judged, were the workings of the mine.

Lukas was studying this through the glasses. Suddenly he handed them to Roger, and said:

'Look straight at the house, then swing slowly towards the mine ... You see the slag heap? ... Yes, good ... Move your glasses downwards very slightly ... Yes?'

Roger moved them. The house seemed to stand on one ledge of rock, and the mine and slag heap on another; a deep valley lay beyond these. In fact, the whole property seemed to stand on a stretch of table-land rather like this one, approached only by the one winding road.

'Yes,' Roger said.

'Now, slowly to the right ... You see the men?'

Roger thought: Men? He forced himself to hold the glasses very steady as he lowered them, and then saw a line of men, tiny even in the binoculars, climbing up the rocky slopes leading to the flat summit. He moved the glasses again and saw another line moving in the same direction, but from another spot. The scene reminded him of the men that he had seen climbing up from the wreckage of the car.

'Who are they?' His voice was tense with excitement, for he believed he knew the answer, and why Lukas and the others had been so amused.

'They are our men, Mr West,' Lukas announced. 'There are two patrols, each with a sergeant and six constables, climbing up. When we give the signal for them to move in, they will move at once. They are local Bantus who know the terrain well. There is no one to match them in the mountains. They are natural guerilla fighters, too, and we have trained them to get the best out of them. You understand we always have to be prepared for trouble in South Africa, and to have a well-trained police force is essential.

Have no fear, Superintendent. If Nightingale and Bradshaw go up there, they will be caught very quickly.'

Roger found himself chuckling.

They turned back towards the camp, and as Roger screwed up his eyes against the sun in one of the clear patches, Hombie called out:

'A car is coming!'

Lukas and Roger ran forward, and scrambled into the larger hole. In the distance a black dot seemed to be moving. In five minutes it had become a blue Humber, moving very fast, throwing up a thick trail of dust. Soon, it passed them. Roger put a pair of binoculars to his eyes, and saw there was only one man at the wheel: Nightingale, driving as if he had not a second to spare.

• • •

An hour and a quarter afterwards, Joshua Bradshaw drove past in a black Chrysler, the car which he had driven from the airport.

• • •

It was like moving forward in a military expedition, a sortie against rebels, perhaps, in the mountains of the Yemen or the hills of Cyprus. The police drove from the lookout camp in two cars, keeping radio contact with the two patrols who had signalled that they were close to the house and the mine, and could move in whenever directed. Roger felt a sense of anticlimax and yet of anxiety. There were murderers in that house. Faith Soames was in their hands, and Nightingale, too. Nightingale must surely believe that he could bring the others to terms, but it might be only a forlorn hope.

And Joshua Bradshaw – what would he do?

Roger wanted above everything else to go forward, into the house, to find out what was going on. The five of them must now be together: Faith, Nightingale, Bradshaw, and the two who might be the Italians Severini and Galli. What had brought them all here with such urgency? Did they know that they were surrounded? Once they found out, what would they do?

The cars pulled up in the shadow of a huge slag heap, a man-made mountain of drab grey, with rough sides covered here and there with dark green, except where it was in the sunlight, where the green seemed as vivid as lichen. Roger and the others got out. Sergeant Hombi moved away, keeping under cover with a skill which told Roger how right Lukas was about the standard of training.

Now there was time to study the position of the house. It stood on a table of land which jutted out from a massive wall of rock, so that it could be approached from two sides and the front, but not from the back. Between the table and the mine-workings there ran a narrow ridge of rock, which seemed to cross a wide ravine, an ugly, jagged mass. Beyond the mines were some long, low-roofed, stone-built buildings, the compound for the mine-workers.

The huge slag heap was fed by a narrow gauge railway with several tracks which were still and silent.

Whether by design or not, the house was in a fine defensive position, and to reach the table of land on which it stood the two patrols had had to climb up on two sides of the rocky slopes. The actual edges of the table were broken by cracks or fissures, some only a foot wide, some several feet.

Roger was still studying the terrain and realizing how difficult the climb had been for the Bantu constables, when Sergeant Hombi came back.

'They are in position and will move in on the signal,' Hombi reported to Lukas.

'Superintendent,' Lukas said to Roger, 'I hope you will wait here until we have completed the raid. As you yourself have said these men are dangerous, and they are armed. It is possible there will be shooting. I would be in serious trouble with my superiors if you were to be hurt. Please stay here.'

Roger thought almost angrily: I've flown all this way, I've taken these chances, they're here because I begged them to come, and they don't want me to be in at the kill. As the thoughts ran through his mind, he looked into Lukas's brown eyes, and saw Hombi, who was so like Jameson, also staring at him. There was no doubt that they were pleading with him to agree, and not to take risks. They would not plead if they could compel him to stay behind.

Everything in his being urged him to reject the pleas, to go to the house with them. He could see their point of view and understand their anxiety; he felt a sense of gratitude, and satisfaction, too, that they should be so anxious and treat him with such solicitude, but – my God, did they think he was made of cotton-wool?

Suddenly, the decision was made for him.

There was a shot from the house; a shout; another shot, followed by a reverberating thud. The front door opened and Nightingale appeared, with Faith just behind him. Nightingale was holding her wrist, as if he were dragging her, but she was running as fast. He turned towards the side of the house, weaving this way and that, and as he did so two men appeared in the doorway – two small men. One of them had a gun poised, and fired twice: there was no way of telling whether either of the fugitives had been hit.

Hombi, Lukas, and the other two Europeans had snatched their revolvers out; there was a fierce rattle of bullets, the two small men seemed to crumple up. As they did so, Nightingale released Faith's hand and staggered forward, knees bending; he had been hit. The girl ran on, skirt riding half-way up her legs, running blindly as if driven only by terror.

Roger bellowed: 'Faith! It's all right! Faith!'

But as he shouted there was a crackle of shooting from the other side of the house, someone must have tried to get away there, and one of the police patrols was in action. It strengthened terror and it added wings to the girl, who was still running blindly.

Roger was already moving towards her, calling as loudly as he could:

'Faith! It's all right. You're safe, safe!'

The word 'safe' seemed to echo about the rocks and the valleys, about the slag heap and the house itself. *S-A-A-A-A-FE.* He thought she heard him. She glanced round. She must have seen some of the armed policemen, Bantus, and they frightened her. She ran straight on, wildly, all control gone. Roger saw which way she was heading, saw that if she wasn't cut off she would fall over the edge of the ravine. He did not pause to reason that the Bantus would be more able than he to save her.

There was a short cut, where the ground was rough, but none of the Bantus was taking it; they were probably worried about the men inside the house. So Roger took it. He thought he heard his name called in a stentorian voice, heard two more shots – and then plunged into a patch of stony ground. Quite suddenly the earth seemed to open up beneath him. As he toppled downwards, he realized with awful certainty what he had done. Here was a jagged tear in the rock, a fissure which ran almost at right angles to the main crevice, and he was falling into it.

Beneath him there was nothing but small stones and jagged rocks and the bottom of the crevice hundreds of feet below. He actually thought: *Hundreds, thousands.* He hunched his body and tried to protect his head with his hands; he felt the pain of blow after blow, against his ribs, his legs, his thighs, his arms, his neck, his head, his hands, his feet. It was as if every part of his body was being assaulted by the rocks, as if they were striking at him viciously, sadistically.

He did not lose consciousness altogether.

He was aware of the pain, and of sounds which happened inside him, as if his bones were breaking. He felt numbness as well as pain. He felt heat. The pain seemed to be drawn from the rest of his body into his head, for his head ached as he had never known it, and was hot, hot, terribly hot, burning hot.

He felt sick, but it was not an intolerable nausea; even his stomach was going numb. But not his head. That was burning. Flaming. He could not move; he could do nothing to cool it.

It so happened that he had fallen where the sun still struck savagely, and where there was no shade.

25

EBB AND FLOW

ROGER WAS aware of sounds.

They were vague sounds. He could not distinguish them. They were accompanied by shadowy movements. Now and again they were accompanied by sharp stabbing pains in his arm – always in his arm. He did not know what caused these. He became aware of a light touch on his forehead, and of something hard in his mouth – they were holding his mouth open, the fools. He did not realize that when he first thought 'the fools', it was the beginning of real consciousness. After that, he knew more about what was going on, although no one spoke to him. It was as if his own mind was slightly below the surface, aware of what was happening but indifferent and uninterested.

Before long, the shapes became less shadowy, and he knew what was happening. He was in hospital. They were doctors and nurses. They were taking his temperature. They were cooling his forehead. They were giving him injections. After every injection he slept for a while, and when he came round from one of them he saw a face. He had seen it before. It was a black face. He thought of Lieutenant Jameson, in London – it was his face. Or was it that sergeant's, whom he had met out on the rocks. Whoever it was smiled, and it was a warming and reassuring smile. A gentle voice said :

'You will soon be well.'

Of course he would ... wouldn't he?

He had a sense that life as well as consciousness was ebbing and flowing. Gradually, the times when it flowed seemed to be longer and the flood-tide stronger. He began to remember things. Suddenly he became anxious for Faith Soames, and soon after he came round again he was even more anxious. And he did not even know what had happened at Van der Lunn's place. Why didn't someone come and tell him?

His anxiety, his curiosity, and his interest ebbed; again nothing mattered. He dozed, and woke, and on waking his mind seemed to be much more its usual self, he saw everything clearly, and when he had lain on his back staring at the venetian blinds at the window, he looked round for a bell. His right arm was stiff, but he could move it. He knew there was something holding his waist and his left leg firmly, but he did not think much about that. He found a bell-push, and pressed, and very soon footsteps sounded, and the door opened and a middle-aged nurse came in, anxious at first, but then beaming all over her pleasant face.

'You're awake!' she cried. 'You'll be all right now.' She spoke as if to reassure herself as much as to reassure him. 'I will fetch the doctor. Don't move, just wait.' She went out bustling, and Roger lay and looked at tiny slats of light which crept through the blinds, and made him remember the fierce heat of the sun.

Two men, white-smocked, came in …

.   .   .

He had been in the main hospital in Johannesburg for five days, he learned at intervals. He had nothing to worry about now, but for a day or two the doctors had been anxious about him. They said so very clearly, so that he should not be tempted to try to overdo it, and so have a relapse. He had fractured his left leg below the knee, a clean break quickly mended, and had cracked some ribs and dislocated his left shoulder, hence all the strapping and the plaster round his leg. His chief danger had been from the effect of the sun; heatstroke. It was unusual for a man to be affected so quickly; had he been run down, or working at too high a pressure? In the quietness of his own mind Roger knew that he had been working at too high a pressure, and so he had been more vulnerable than he should have been.

What about Nightingale? And the girl? And …

Some time afterwards, Captain Standish appeared at the bedside, instead of the doctors. He looked as sardonic and as cynical as ever, but the grip of his hand on Roger's uninjured right hand gave the lie to much of that.

'Just like the Yard,' he said. 'You couldn't leave it to anyone else. Did anyone take the trouble to tell you that the young woman saw you fall? That made her stop, or she would have gone down herself.'

'It's a charitable thought,' said Roger. 'Really?'

'Cross my heart.' Standish almost leered. 'Nightingale was shot in the back, but the bullet is out and he'll be all right, which a lot of people think is more than he deserves.'

'Do I deserve to be told whether he's made a statement?' asked Roger.

'Yes, he has, and so has the young woman,' Standish said. 'Nightingale was sure that the Bradshaws were involved. He believed that Faith Soames had been kidnapped, so that the kidnappers could blackmail him and prevent him from telling the police what he knew of the Bradshaws – and he went to save her. He was not so reckless as you might think, though. He had sent a coded cable to old Soames's private address, giving all the details of his case against the Bradshaws – both the brothers, not one. He went to the mine prepared to say that if the girl was freed Soames would not publish the story – he was sure that Soames would back him up. That's why he felt that he could safely tackle the people at the mine. We now know that David Bradshaw had bribed porters at most airports. There was one at the Jan Smuts, a man who also worked for the brother, and put the diamonds into Nightingale's luggage. Now, what's next? Ah, yes. Faith Soames had a telephone call from a man who said that he was *The Globe*'s reporter in Johannesburg, so she went to meet him. I suppose she can't be blamed for that. She arranged to meet the car in Kempton Park, but drove past it to see who was at the wheel, and realized that it wasn't *The Globe* man at all. So she tried to get away, but they shot at her car and punctured a tyre. She reached the telephone kiosk and made that call to you, after distracting them by driving the car up a side-street. They chased after it. She slipped back to the telephone, but they caught up with her too soon. When Nightingale heard that she was a prisoner he went to try to do a deal at Van der Lunn's place. He told them that the story about Van der Lunn was already in London, but they didn't seem to care.' Standish's lip twisted. 'Guess why.'

Roger said quietly: 'Because Van der Lunn wasn't involved.'

'You never were convinced of that, were you?'

'No,' said Roger. 'I was mistaken about the Bradshaws, but not about Van der Lunn. The thefts and the smuggling seemed big, but not big enough for a man of his reputation to risk losing it, or for a patriotic South African to cheat his Government.'

'I know how you get results,' said Standish. 'You make a wild guess and then justify it by logic. Feel like guessing what was really going on?'

Roger said: 'You tell me.'

'Like to sleep on it, and guess tomorrow?'

'I'll sleep on it when you've told me what it was,' said Roger. When Standish didn't respond, he went on: 'If you must play your little game, it's now obvious that both the Bradshaws were involved, and that when we arrested David Bradshaw, either the accomplices or Joshua Bradshaw believed he would tell us the whole truth, so they killed him.'

'Cain and Abel?'

'Was it?'

'Yes,' said Standish. 'He had more reason than you might think, though. David's wife didn't know that Joshua was involved, but she believed her husband was under pressure. She meant to make him talk – the one thing Joshua feared. But Joshua swears he didn't order the killing in the police-station – the Italians planned that themselves, convinced that David *would* give them away.' Standish pushed his chair back and stood up, as if he did not intend to tell Roger any more yet, but all he did was to call out: 'Come in, Lieutenant.' The door opened and Jameson came in, smiling and obviously contented; so it was his, not Hombi's face Roger had seen in his half-conscious state. Jameson came across, shook hands, and stood back from the bed. Standish remained on his feet, too.

'I am very glad you are not worse,' said Jameson, as if that mattered more than anything else. 'And I congratulate you, Superintendent. I have been told that but for your bravery much more harm might have been done. However, I am here to report what happened in England. First I bring you a message from your wife, whom I saw two days ago. Her love. Next, I bring you the regards of the Assistant Commissioner' – he paused – 'Chief Inspectors Klemm and McKay, and Detective-Sergeant Gorlay. All of them are very gratified by the result. The others who worked with the team also send their best wishes, Superintendent.'

'This team-work,' interpolated Standish.

'That was the strongest impression made on me by Scotland Yard – the close integration of all the departments and all the ranks,' said Jameson. 'Since the arrest of Joshua Bradshaw, who was not hurt but was caught when hiding from the police, Rebecca Bradshaw and Elizabeth Bradshaw have made full statements. They did not know what was afoot, but were afraid it was criminal, and tried to stop their husbands going on with it. They were going to leave the hotel very soon. Each woman trusted and loved her husband, there's no doubt about that.'

'And Joshua?'

'Joshua has confessed to everything except a part in his brother's murder. The Bradshaw's worked with the two Italians who spent much time at the Seven Seas Club in Soho. That was the place of contact, an unofficial headquarters. Common View Hotel was kept simply as a cover. All arrangements were made by telephone and by word of mouth. The story which David Bradshaw told us was untrue, of course – he and his brother were the organizers of the smuggling – and they used the Italians to go to the industrial users and steal the diamonds back. Apart from porters at each airport, men who once persuaded to commit a crime could thereafter be blackmailed into doing whatever they were told, no one else was involved.' Jameson glanced at Standish. 'Have you informed Mr West of the Van der Lunn aspect of the situation, Captain?'

'No,' said Standish promptly. 'I was hoping he would

guess. I think it would be good for his ego. Going to have a shot, Handsome?'

It was the first time he had used the nickname.

Roger said almost musingly: 'Van der Lunn wasn't guilty, but suddenly he became a danger to them. So, he must have found out what was going on. However, he couldn't have found out until he was on the aircraft or he would have telephoned the police. He must have seen something at the Jan Smuts, and faced David Bradshaw with it. Bradshaw took immediate action, putting drugs in his drinks – morphine kept on the plane for emergencies in flight. How am I doing?'

Standish said: 'Too well!'

'There is more,' Jameson said.

'There must be much more,' Roger agreed. 'Well, let's see.' He was beginning to feel tired, and rather edgy. It would be interesting to find out how far he could interpret the events in the light of what information he now had. He leaned back on his pillows, closing his eyes, letting thoughts and the new facts drift through his mind rather than making any effort at logical thought; this was the way he worked whenever there was a case without an obvious solution. At last he went on: 'So Van der Lunn found out and had to be silenced, but David Bradshaw didn't want him dead. David was not prepared to commit murder. Actually, he *saved* Van der Lunn's life at the hotel, and the Italians knew this – another reason for the daring murder. They had needed his mine, and all the facilities which only a mine could offer.'

Jameson was beaming, Standish smiling wryly.

'Just a little more,' Jameson urged. 'You are so very near. May I give him a hint, Captain?'

'A very little one.'

'A little hint,' Jameson said. 'Yes.' He paused, and then added: 'Traffic moves in two directions, Superintendent.'

Standish chuckled.

'That's good,' he said. 'And that's all. How about it, Handsome?'

26

TRAFFIC FLOWS TWO WAYS

AFTER A long pause, Roger said: 'No, I don't get it.' He was much more tired than he had expected, and his eagerness to know the final truth was less sharp than it had been; he wanted to know, but he was half-prepared to wait until morning. 'Traffic moves two ways,' he said aloud. 'No. You'll have to tell me.'

As he spoke the door opened and two nurses came in, one of them indignant, the other apologetic. The Superintendent had already been talking too long, and in any case, the doctor was on his way to see him. Standish stood up, Jameson seemed to hesitate, and then Standish said:

'Will you sleep on it?'

'I think I'd better.'

He thought about it a great deal. A two-way traffic. There must be a simple answer, and yet it didn't come to him. It teased but did not worry him. In any case, it could not stop him from sleeping, for they gave him an injection and he was wafted off within ten minutes. Before he slept he thought of the 'two-way traffic' and half-consciously about the message from Janet. It would be good to see her, to get back.

In the morning, he felt much better than he had done since coming round. He felt hungrier, and believed that he could walk if it weren't for the plaster about his leg. He was impatient for Standish and Jameson to come again, too, and when they didn't arrive by eleven o'clock, he began to feel annoyed. That did not last long. He sensed from the way the nurses fussed that there was a special visitor about to come, probably the specialist who had been consulted. Instead, Colonel Wiess came in by himself. This was really the top treatment.

Wiess saluted, shook hands, smiled down, pulled up a chair, and said:

'Two-way traffic, Superintendent?'

'I haven't got the answer,' Roger said.

'It would have been only a matter of time,' Wiess said. 'And it is very simple. We were searching for a method of smuggling diamonds into foreign countries after they had left South Africa, but passengers were seldom found with diamonds in their baggage. We were looking at the wrong end. The diamonds were being smuggled out, sold, stolen, and—'

'Smuggled back into South Africa!' Roger cried.

'Ach, yes, that is sø. They were then put into stock at the Van der Lunn's mine, and eventually sold to de Beers and the Syndicate, who believed that they had been newly mined here in South Africa. The two Italians and Joshua Bradshaw went to the mine to steal a large stock of diamonds they knew were there. The fraud was connived at by Mr Van der Lunn's managers. We have confronted his managers with this, and they have admitted it. We know what happened to him when he reached London – in fact, what happened from the time he boarded the aircraft.' Wiess paused, and then added in a gruff voice: 'There is no need to involve him.'

Roger said slowly: 'So it all works out.'

'Yes,' said Wiess. 'It has worked out so quickly because you came to South Africa. I know that I speak for many people as well as myself when I say that I am very grateful indeed.'

Roger asked, quietly: 'Even Nightingale and Miss Soames?'

For the first time in Roger's knowledge of him, Wiess actually threw back his head and laughed.

'Only this morning copies of The Globe reached us by air-mail,' he said. 'I have one for you.' He opened his briefcase and handed Roger the *Daily Globe*, folded so that the front page was hidden. He opened it, and saw the banner head-lines:

SA TRIUMPH FOR 'HANDSOME' WEST

There was his photograph, and Faith's, and Nightingale's. There was a story, told forthrightly and clearly, giving nothing away that was best kept secret and yet telling everything that mattered. Roger was so intent on it that although he saw Wiess move he did not realize that the Colonel had gone to the door. He was just aware that the door had opened, thought vaguely that Wiess must be allowing him to enjoy his triumph in peace, saw an arrow pointing from a sentence in italics: *West's Wife and Family – p. 7.* He turned to page seven, and Janet and the boys were there, smiling as if straight at him. Janet was looking her best, the boys apparently as happy as could be.

Someone was standing by the bedside. It wasn't Wiess, it was a woman. He looked up. He gaped. He gasped. He could not believe it, but there she was: Janet, his wife, standing and looking down on him, smiling a little tremulously but smiling. More: she was looking quite at her best, better even than in the photograph.

Suddenly she was leaning over him, and kissing him, and crying a little. Tears did not last for long, and she drew back and sat on the side of the bed. She kept a hand on his arm, lightly, and looked at him as if hungrily.

'We're all so proud of you, darling. So very proud.' She gave an excited little laugh. 'All of us. Soames of *The Globe* telephoned me and said enough to make you blush. And his niece – isn't she charming? – came and saw me as soon as she got back to London. She said she never expected to meet a more remarkable man. She thinks so much of you. Roger, darling, I was so afraid before you went away; I thought you'd got tired of me. I thought you'd fallen in love with another woman. And Faith Soames said that all you seemed to talk about, when she met you here, was me.'

JOHN CREASEY

OF THE few men who can be called a legend in their own lifetime, John Creasey is undeniably in the front rank. Anyone who meets this tall, solidly-built man soon becomes aware of his driving vitality, which is largely responsible for his amazing achievements, his strong opinions on a wide variety of subjects, and his determination not only to make himself heard but also to make whatever he writes better year by year.

After receiving over 700 rejection slips ('All deserved,' he will say), he has published over 450 books, or more than 40 million words, which have sold some 50 million copies and are now selling at the rate of 4 millions a year in twenty-five different languages. He has had books serialized, as well as adapted for radio and television, all over the world. Statistically he is truly something of a wonder.

Some critics now realize that the quality of his recent work has been as remarkable as its quantity. Writing in the *New York Times* Mr Anthony Boucher said: 'Creasey is creating his own kind of *comédie humaine policière*, and a splendid achievement it is.' Dr Felix Marti-Ibanez says: 'He is writing a Balzacian human comedy depicting the mores, and above all the violence, of our times; each book acquires a new and wider perspective when seen as a fragment of a gigantic literary canvas.'

The *Daily Express* reports that he prefers 'the girl-next-door' sort of woman. His favourite colours are fresh greens and yellows; favourite dresses utterly simple.

He lives rather palatially near Salisbury with his wife Jean and sons Martin, an art student, and Richard, who works at the television studios, Elstree. He travels widely, not only to make sure that his local colour is accurate but also to see his publishers, editors, and agents throughout the world. He drinks no alcohol, is a pioneer Road Safety man, chairman of the local Oxfam Committee, sighs for the great days of English cricket, and is quite sure the British Commonwealth is a much underrated institution.

What the critics say about John Creasey:

'You can always rely on the phenomenal Creasey.'

The Observer.

'Excitement is confidently expected from Mr Creasey.'
and
'There may come a time when all the possibilities of crime fiction will have been fully explored. Mr Creasey's inventive powers make that prospect seem remote.'

The Times Literary Supplement.

'John Creasey must be the nearest thing to perpetual motion that we have in crime-fiction writing. Regularly a new mystery thriller comes along – and there's always a new twist and dramatic plot to keep one's interest unflaggingly held.'

Manchester Evening News